WINDOWS OF THE SOUL

First edition. April 19, 2024.

Copyright © 2024 Jayce Hitten.

ISBN: 979-8224097616

Written by Jayce Hitten.

Table of Contents

Windows of the Soul
Anthology of Life's Final Moments
By: Jayce Hitten
Inspired by Fred Pirlot's "In an Open Eye" Artwork

Acknowledgements:

I extend my heartfelt gratitude to Fred Pirlot, whose profound influence and inspiration catalyzed the creation of this anthology. The beginning of this literary journey can be traced back to his evocative print, "In an Open Eye," a work of art that not only sparked my creative spirit but also became an integral part of the cover art for this collection. The print served as the catalyst for the narrative titled "Oppression," intimately connected to the poignant story of Shaima al-Sabbagh, who tragically lost her life during a protest in Egypt. Fred's generosity in granting permission to use "In an Open Eye" as part of the cover art is a testament to his support and encouragement throughout this creative endeavor.

The inception of this anthology unfolded during a profound moment of reflection. Upon encountering "In an Open Eye" for the first time, the image stirred memories of Shaima al-Sabbagh, prompting the birth of the story of "Oppression" and the symbolic layers that followed. Following this powerful encounter, I retreated to my hotel room, compelled to lay out the initial outline for the stories encapsulated in this book. While many ideas originated from the reservoir of general knowledge amassed over a lifetime, they underwent meticulous refinement through years of dedicated research, a process that infused depth and authenticity into the narratives. The concepts for each story may have laid dormant for a while, but the overarching idea for this anthology remained a constant presence in my thoughts, continuously refreshed by ongoing inspirations drawn from personal interactions, encounters, and the diverse array of stories and books that crossed my path.

This anthology, therefore, stands as a testament to the enduring impact of Fred Pirlot's inspiration and the multitude of influences that have shaped its narrative landscape. It is a reflection of the collective reservoir of human experiences, both personal and observed, meticulously woven together to create a tapestry of stories that resonate with authenticity and meaning. I am deeply thankful for the invaluable contributions of those who have played a role in this creative odyssey, and I look forward to sharing these tales with the world.

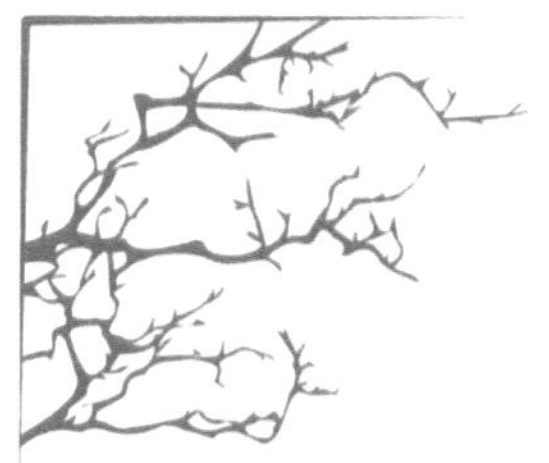

Forward:

In my search for inspiration for my writing I travel to museums, parks, art galleries, surf the web, read, and research articles, magazines, and books, and many other methods. This anthology is no different. In fact, this anthology was created solely based on Fred Pirlot's "In an Open Eye" print I found while walking through the various art galleries in downtown Savannah Georgia in 2014. From that single print it spawned over half the story ideas immediately and the rest of the stories continued to develop as I began to write down the ideas.

We hear the adage of how "the eyes are the windows of the soul" throughout our lives and while we hear the stories of what people believe is seen upon death through either science, religion, or personal belief I have never personally seen anyone attempt to bring together these various beliefs. Even though I am Christian in faith I have studied other faiths as part of my writing and do not claim myself an expert, I attempt to present different perspectives that I have found through my research. I cannot possibly discuss every such scenario from every aspect, but I do try to highlight the most prominent that I have found.

Additionally, with the discussion of death this anthology may trigger some unwanted feelings. As a former soldier that served my entire career in a time of war and lost many friends to combat, suicide, cancer and other illnesses, and accidents as well as family members I have learned to embrace death and my faith has taught me that life and even death is a time for celebration and not sorrow. That there is always a way to find solace and peace in the passing of a loved one in time. That does not mean I do not grieve, because I do. It also does not mean I believe all of which I have written within these pages or support the ideas but have written them once again based on personal beliefs, religious beliefs, and scientific beliefs that I have researched. I cannot emphasize that enough.

I also do not wish to romanticize nor condone the taking of one's life. I have lost too many friends to suicide and if you may be feeling the urge to do so I strongly encourage you to seek help from those around you or the diverse services available. Your life is precious, and you bring joy to those around you more than you could ever imagine. Listed below are some services available should you or someone you know need assistance. I am not affiliated with any of the services listed but support their efforts in getting help and assistance to those in need.

National Suicide Prevention Hotline: 1-800-273-8255 or text 988 for the crisis text line.

https://save.org
https://AFSP.org
https://www.sprc.org
https://www.nomv.org
https://www.veteranscrisisline.net
https://www.militaryveteranproject.org

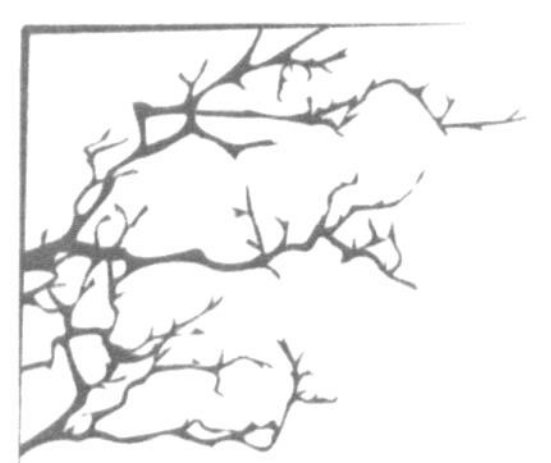

The Departure

A heart rate monitor beeped steadily as the doctor reassured Anna that everything was going well. Looking over at her husband, Robert, she managed a strained smile as he maintained his grip on her hand. Her face glistened, and her hair was matted with sweat that accumulated over the past couple of hours of labor. She grit her teeth as she braced for another push, barely able to feel due to the epidural. The monitor began to beep a bit more rapidly, which it had been doing on and off throughout her ordeal.

"You're doing great, the baby's crowning." The doctor stated calmly as the nurse encouraged Anna to push again.

In a moment of respite between contractions, Anna looked into Robert's eyes and whispered softly, "We've been through so much... I just want our baby to be safe." Her voice quivered with determination and love as she found strength in her desire to bring her child into the world. It became clear that her unwavering dedication stemmed from her deep-rooted maternal instincts and unconditional love for their unborn baby. Her breath caught as it became time to push once again.

Straining against the numbness she pushed again tightly, closing her eyes welcoming the peace of the stillness in the darkness behind her eyelids. She heard the doctor say that the baby's head is now out and is asked for one final push. Reaching inward for strength her eyes shutting tighter, her nose scrunching up, and a toothy joyless grin split her mouth as the heart rate monitor raced, before letting out a scream.

After another round of intense pushing, Anna made one last effort as Robert squeezed her hand tightly. With a rush of relief and joy, their baby was pulled free and brought into the world. Anna fell back into the bed as the umbilical cord was cut and handed off to the awaiting nurse.

The doctor followed the nurse taking the baby to the far side of the room to perform post birthing checks. Feeling exhausted she rolled her head to the side as the heart monitor's pace began to normalize. She took in the vision of her husband through teary eyes and smiled at him.

He looked down at her, smiling, still holding her hand as the murmuring of the doctor and nurses caught his attention. He eyed the doctor and nurses with a look of concern on his face. Anna tried to raise her head to glance over and found it difficult to do so. Robert looked down at her, a worried expression on his face, as she softly spoke.

"I don't feel right." Anna's eyes rolled back into her head as her hand holding his went limp. Robert quickly released her hand and took her head in his hands pleading with her to look at him. Anna heard his voice calling to her but through her diminishing sight it began to fade. The sound of the heart monitor beeping became erratic and though fading it was deafening. Unable to control herself her body began to convulse as she lost consciousness.

Time stood still as Anna lost herself in the darkness. Everything around her transformed into chaos, and though she was unable to see anything, she sensed the tension enveloping her surroundings. Sounds of her husband shouting, the doctor giving orders, the heart rate monitor beeping all came at her as muffled echoes. She felt cold in the darkness as someone pushed against her abdomen and pelvic region.

Though the feeling was forceful it all felt numb as if her body had fallen asleep. It was like a foot you sat on too long folded in your lap only it would not wake. Only she did not feel the sensation of pins and needles she expected to come. Unable to move or speak or see or barely even feel she thought she must be dreaming until the fading sounds around her went silent.

Only a moment had passed when Anna opened her eyes and found herself floating above her motionless body. The muffled voices of the doctor, nurses, and Robert left a distant echo in her mind. A pool of blood had formed at her waist on the birthing table and spilled onto the floor as a nurse assisted the doctor with gauze as he held a spare set of sterile forceps at the ready.

Her husband was being forced out of the delivery room by another nurse when two orderlies met him on the other side. Standing outside the doors as they slowly flapped closed, tears began filling his eyes and concern blanketed his face. Anna attempted to move toward him but was unable to shift her elevated position above her body. The heart monitor flashed quick peaks among the various indicator lines as the doctor and nurses worked through the discord.

Gazing to the corner of the room where they took her baby, she saw another nurse worked to clear obstructions from the baby's mouth and was beginning procedures to resuscitate the lifeless form. Unable to contain herself, Anna screamed only to find no sound being produced.

She wailed silently as she watched with intent at the nurse and tried stretching her hands out trying to reach her child. She struggled, unable to move from her floating position, frozen in place failing to move any closer. Helplessness filled her as she hovered in the air incapable to provide for her child.

The room became brighter unexpectedly as if someone had turned on more lights centered in the room above Anna. A light like natural sunlight with an orange glow unlike the hospital lights already alight in the room. Examining the room, the nurses and doctor were nowhere near the wall switches and her husband was still standing outside the doors with the orderlies. Turning her head in her suspended position, she looked around in the room unsure of who could have turned on the light. Gazing up towards the ceiling she realized why.

The light engulfed the ceiling, or rather where the ceiling had been. Beaming down from a distant point far into the sky, it was radiant and inviting. The light swirled to form a tunnel out of varied hues of brilliance. From the far point a twinkling beacon began to fall towards Anna through the vastness of light. As the beacon made its way towards her, Anna realizes that she herself was also beginning to be lifted into the light. While she maintained control of her body as she floated, she lacked control over her ascent into the light.

Anna began to struggle, fighting against her rising body, trying to grasp at objects within her reach. Her hands and fingers passed through the IV stand, the top of the birthing table, the power cables connected to the wall for the heart monitor and other devices. She frantically tried to stay afloat above her own lifeless body in order to stay with her baby, her husband, her body. Slowly she continued to ascend into the illuminated corridor, still looking down into the hospital room trying to grab objects as she moved higher and higher.

She rose high enough now that the whole room was visible without having to turn. The doctor and nurse still working frantically to stop her bleeding, the nurse in the corner tirelessly trying to bring life into her child. Her husband was no longer within her sight at this angle. An overwhelming urge to scream gripped her in frustration at the struggle, if only she were able to.

As Anna looked up into the light, the powerful force continued to pull at her as if beckoning her into the light. She tried to resist more, desperately trying to cling onto the lights as her hands passed through them. No matter how hard she struggled, the pull became stronger and stronger.

Panic began to set in as the feeling of the force and her resistance began to feel as if she could be torn apart. No one in the room noticed Anna struggling while focusing on their tasks at hand as the unseen power kept her from returning.

As she rose higher her husband was visible on the other side of the room. Outside the doors, he looked as though he sensed something was wrong. He watched on distraught, as orderlies held him back while he screamed silently for someone to save his wife. Time ticked away as Anna was forced closer and closer towards the blinding light and chaos reigned as everyone involved were in fights against forces beyond their understanding or control.

Helpless, she closed her eyes to cry, but nothing happened. Unable to do anything for her child, to comfort her husband, she stopped fighting. A twinkling light beyond her closed eyes caused her to open her eyes and saw a shimmering golden mass floating before her. Formless, its mass moved slowly toward Anna. Using caution, she put her hand up guarding herself from its approach.

As the shimmering light started to envelop her hand, an overwhelming sense of happiness and love surged within her. Despite the absence of a visible face, physical touch, or audible voice, she recognized the glowing essence as her child. The unfolding event bewildered her, yet the soothing sensation emanating from the light eased her apprehensions. Sensing her child's pure and affectionate soul, she felt embraced by its love as the light swirled around her.

Though unable to form words in her mouth Anna still mouthed "I love you" as the golden form fell away into the hospital room below. No longer filled with dread, she watched as the light illuminated the table in front of the nurse resuscitating her child.

In moments she could see her baby open her eyes as it was filled with life. Smiling, she stopped resisting the ascent and realized the light held warmth and she could now hear beautiful music growing louder. No longer fighting the immense force pulling her, she let go of her fear and accepted what was to come. Gazing deep into the light she slowly vanished among its intensity.

1:11-A:B:E:K

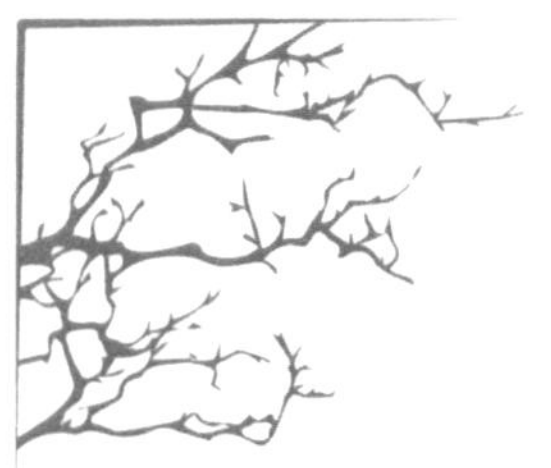

Reminiscence

He fiddled with the pill bottle with arthritic hands, unable to get the cap loose for several minutes. Brandon sat up in bed and tossed his book aside. Frowning at it he realized he had closed it without leaving a dog ear on a corner to mark his place.

Standing up the symphony of cracking bones echoed in his room as he stood as straight as possible reaching over and putting the pill bottle down on his bed. Knowing he would not be able to get to sleep without his pill he decided to take a walk before settling down for the evening now that he had failed to open his pills and enjoy his own reading adventure.

Crossing the room, he grabbed his robe from off the wooden peg built into the door and donned it as he opened the door letting the light from his room flood the dark hallway. He stepped into his slippers and shuffled into the halls of the Everest Retirement Home.

The corridor was silent much like the rooms lining the hallway as most residents had gone to sleep already. Even though he could not see any at the moment he knew the nurses on duty would be making their rounds throughout the evening to those that required more frequent care, but for now the halls remained still.

The plain white walls of the corridor opened into the main foyer where a fire burned in the large stone hearth. Feeling a little winded from his walk, Brandon decided to sit in a chair near the fire to relax. Staring into the flames he let his mind drift as they danced among the logs.

The smell of the natural logs burning filled his nostrils with smells reminiscent of when he used to go camping. He had not been sitting more than five minutes when he heard the sneakered steps of one of the nurses on duty approaching him from behind. They were sure to scold him for being up so late.

"And what are you doing up so late?" A soft voice asked as a shapely woman in her thirties with shoulder length strawberry blonde hair framing a pale face rounded the side of his chair. Her blue eyes peered at him from behind black rectangularly framed glasses quizzically as a small smile curled her lips.

"Oh, I couldn't sleep." Brandon mumbled. He knew she was going to scold him. "I just came out here to relax some before trying to get to sleep again. Are you going to take me away to my room now?"

"Take you away? No, not right now. I saw you out here by yourself and thought I'd join you if that is all right."

"That'd be fine. Have a seat. Are you new here? You look familiar, but I don't recall your name. I apologize sometimes my memory isn't that good anymore."

"Of course, you know me, Brandon. My names...are you ok?" She began to stand in order to provide him with aid as he winced in obvious discomfort grabbing at his forehead.

"I'm ok. It's just a little headache. Please sit. I'll be fine, really." He started waving at her to sit as he rubbed his eyes. "I'm sorry, you were saying?"

"Just call me nurse if it makes it easier for you." She stated to ease his frustration. "Well Brandon, what would you like to talk about?"

"Oh, I don't know. What would you like to know? I may not be able to remember what I had for breakfast most days, but I remember pretty much of what I've done in my life if you care to hear that. It's all I care to know anyhow The damned tv only shows bad news, I stopped paying attention to that a long time ago."

"Call me old fashioned sweety, but I do enjoy everyone's life stories here. So, what's yours?"

"Oh, not really much to tell." He muttered shrugging his shoulders. "Simple childhood, joined the military, was a mailman, fell in love, got married, had a family, lost my wife, raised our kids, got old, and ended up here. Pretty simple."

"No, no, no. you can't tell it like that." She argued. "You need to add the details."

"Ha!" He laughed. "You remind me of my wife. She always wanted the details when it came to everything. Especially with how my day went, even though it was the same thing over and over as a mail man."

"Sounds like her and I'd be fast friends." She stared at him with intent. "Well? The details?"

"She'd like that. Ok. Well like I said my childhood was pretty simple. I liked to play video games. I was also extremely interested in space and have always wanted to go. Which, I guess is why I joined the Air Force. I figured that may be the best chance, but my job wasn't the most exciting. Can't do many exciting things in the Air Force from a middle of nowhere base in New Mexico."

"No, I suppose not." She agreed. "Thank you for your service regardless. How long did you serve?"

"Oh, not long. It wasn't for me. I got out, moved back home, and worked a few odd jobs before I settled on working as a mail carrier. I did that for thirty years. That's actually when I met up with my future wife."

"You met your wife on your mail route? That's not creepy at all." She teased as she got up and moved over to a table by the fireplace to pour a couple glasses of water before returning to the table.

"What? No. We didn't meet, but met back up with each other. We had actually been in high school together though she was slightly older, and we were just friends back then. It wasn't until I came back from being in the military and ran into her again that I even thought about trying to date her. She had been divorced and unfortunately was in a relationship with someone else so I couldn't act on feelings that I had had for her for some time."

"Oooh, I love drama. You did have an interesting life. What was her name?"

"Her name was Tero. She was the most amazing woman." He began to smile, and his eyes grew with excitement as he began to talk about her. "She was working as a nurse when I first got back. Sadly, I cannot recall her face in my memory anymore. But I do have a picture in my room to remind me."

"That's awful. It must be difficult for you."

"It is at times, but I remember her features like her hair, it's similar to yours." He said pointing. "How she always worried about things. How she loved me and our children. She had already had two lovely children, when we got together. I quickly came to love and adore them as my own."

"Would you tell me about them? What are they doing now?"

"The kids? Oh, well after we got together the kids were still young and well, we got pregnant also and had a baby girl of our own before getting married. However, that didn't stop me from falling for all three of them. Lucas ended up joining the military like I did after high school and served eight years and became a teacher. He still teaches, he loves it, in fact it prompted him to follow one of his childhood dreams and now drives a school bus as well."

"Kaelyn has always been a firecracker. She bartended her way through college and law school and is now a partner for a firm in Indianapolis. She's got a serious boyfriend but has yet to marry or have any children. Always been focused on her career."

"Bristol took after her mother and loved all things related to the United Kingdom from Manchester United to Stone Henge, Big Ben, and Sherlock Holmes. She even married a British man who paid her way through vet school. They run a vet clinic together in Sussex. I don't see her often, but she always sends her love and pictures of her family."

Brandon continued for the next thirty minutes recalling sporting events, dance and gymnastic events, family pets, science fairs and projects, relationships and life accomplishments and struggles that they had gone through. He laughed recalling a particularly failed attempt at camping causing the nurse to join in with her own laughter. Every-so-often he struggled with a detail, as he struggled it was always followed by a wince of pain in his head but continued his storytelling regardless of the pain.

"They all sound amazing. I'm sure you both were immensely proud of them." She stated.

"Tero, didn't see them out of high school." He mumbled softly.

"I'm so sorry. I didn't mean to..."

"You didn't know, it's all right. Besides, it's been a long time now. We lost her in a car accident. She really loved that old jeep." He said smiling. "She'd drive it around everywhere waiting for an opportunity to give the 'jeep' wave or pass out a duck. I never did understand that tradition. She kept a bag of them with her at all times." He turned his head away as he thumbed away tears forming in his eyes.

"I've done it again. I'm so sorry." She apologized once again.

"Again?" He puzzled. "I don't recall you bringing up anything before."

"You're too sweet Brandon." She mused in a light voice. "We've had this same conversation, or at least similar ones like it many times now. More times recently. Almost nightly."

He stared at her for a moment. "Well, if that's the case I suppose I should go take my medication."

"If you insist. Then, it's time to go." She smiled as she stood up and then helped him to his feet. "Let's go then."

He groaned as his body ached getting back to his feet. He paused as he realized he would need her help to get back to his room. "Alright. I suppose it is getting late and you probably have other patients to attend to."

"Just you for now." She said as they moved down the hall retreating away from the warmth of the fireplace.

The walk back to his room seemed to be shorter than his initial venture to the main hall. Before he realized it, they reached his room and Brandon thought if his mind had wandered off as he did not recall seeing any other nurses again on the walk back. Opening his room door made him think differently as his bed was made and his book and the pill bottle were resting on his nightstand. He thought to himself that another one of the nurses must have tended to it while he was out.

"Here we are." She must have taken note of his medication as she led him inside and helped him out of his robe hanging it on the door peg. "Go lie down and I'll get that pill for you."

Moving over to the bed and sitting down turning towards the nightstand, he realized he had no water. "Ah, damn. I'm out of water. I need to fill my pitcher." He grumbled. Breaking his pleasant demeanor, he had been portraying since he started talking to the nurse.

"Oh, quit yo bitchin'!" She snapped right back. Placing her hand on her hip she glared at him smiling.

"What did you say?" He was half surprised by the sudden retort from her, but also by the phrase that she used.

"I said, quit yo bitchin', Brandon!"

"Where did you hear that? How do you..." He trailed off puzzled by her smiling at him. "My wife and I used to say that to each other."

"I know Brandon." Still staring at him.

"Oh, right. I've told you before."

"No dummy. It's me, Tero! I swear you are quite thick in your old age."

"Uhm...you do remind me of her, but you can't be."

"Oh seriously?" Moving over to the bed she picks up the picture and held it up against her cheek. "How's this?"

"Tero?" Unable to contain his tears he reached forward and wrapped his arms around her in a loving embrace. Their embrace stopped time as it seemed to drag on forever. Reluctantly he finally released her. "How?"

"Like I said, I've heard your story many times now. You just can't remember. Sometimes you remember what I look like and swear I'm a long lost relative, other times you can't remember my name or our children's names, but you always remember how we met and how our children turned out. I love hearing that part. Especially, Lucas becoming a bus driver. That cracks me up." she said with a wry grin.

"Yes, but how? Why..." he stammered trying to get more words out.

"Up until now I didn't know, but I do now. It's time. You asked earlier if I was here to take you away. It wasn't time then, but it is now. If I had to guess, I would say an aneurysm by the way you keep wincing at a pain in your head."

"What about the kids?"

She smiled and once again repeated. "Will you quit yo bitchin? They are going to be fine. You have taken loving care of them all of their lives, and they have grown into responsible adults that took care of you and have their own families to take care of now. It's time to let go."

"You always were a firecracker when you wanted to be." He said.

"Oh, you're not bringing that old thing. Leave it on the bed."

Slightly confused, but at her request he laid down on the bed and slowly rose up a younger version of himself. Looking down at the bed he gazed down on his older self with his eyes closed as if asleep. A book resting on his chest with the spine up depicting a worn title. He turned around fearful that Tero had vanished only to see her still standing in the center of his room.

"Was that all a dream?"

"In a sense." She said. "But it no longer matters. Are you ready to go?"

"Where are we going?"

"Anywhere, but first, how about space? Haven't you always wanted to go?"

Smiling, he took her hand as they turned to his corner closet. The door opened into a vast starlit sky with a million cosmic features filling their vision. They stepped in together and vanished amongst the vastness as a nurse ran into his room in an attempt to provide aid to the lifeless husk still lying in his bed.

4-XI-D:G:K

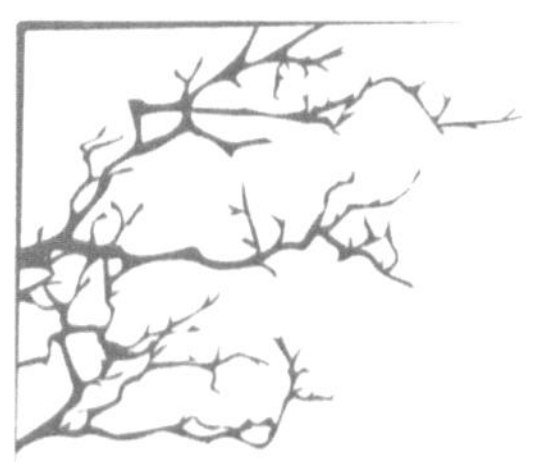

The Vanguard

The heat of the day bared down on Mark as he once again wiped the sweat dripping down into his eyes from his camouflaged face. His hand wiped away the perspiration with ease but came away with a mixture of green and black face paint. Noting the smudge, he made a mental check that he will need to reapply more camo to the area next time they conduct a halt. Absently, he patted his breast pocket where the camo-stick was stashed ensuring it was still in its place.

Keeping his eyes ahead he scanned the area for possible enemy forces lying in ambush as his small element made their way through the dense and dimly lit jungle. The sounds of the night birds, animals, and insects echoed through the trees helped mask the sound of the men moving through the brush despite the slow pace.

His team moved cautiously avoiding dry leaves and sticks so as to not alert the enemy of their location. Though the task was not too difficult with the constant rains, it had been two days since the last. The humidity did well to keep the ground moist, but it did nothing for the dead branches that lie unseen in the underbrush of the thick grass and large leaves that blanketed the jungle floor.

Mark had been sent over to Vietnam three times now. This time he had been able to be part of the elite MACV-SOG unit due to his aptitude to survive from his previous deployments and ability to adapt to the environment. The unit executed strategic reconnaissance missions deep within enemy territory, accomplishing a diverse range of objectives beyond the capabilities of conventional units, despite their numerical challenges of personnel.

This mission was no different. It involved a reconnoiter of an enemy encampment, suspected to be a prisoner of war camp, to conduct a future raid on once more information was gathered. Their job was simple: find the camp, observe for 24-48 hours, and get out. No need to make contact with the enemy, attempt to rescue any POWs, kill as many Vietcong as possible, or any other combination of irrational behavior that could get them killed for no reason.

No one wanted to be a hero, and no one was looking to be one. Each man knew what they were there to do and kept that focus on the tasks at hand. The small team of five men had been infiltrating to this location for three nights now and would be nearing the objective soon Mark thought. In the jungle your senses became heightened, especially when another was not able to be used, in this case their eyesight.

While the moon should be full and bright in the sky the light barely made it through the triple canopy. The men had to rely on their other senses to help guide them through the labyrinth of trees and grass. Vines, leaves, and mud made their journey dangerous with the sounds they could make and the possible missteps tripping them up.

All of a sudden, Mark saw movement to his immediate eleven o'clock. He narrowed his eyes and raised his rifle quickly flowing from the low ready to the rigid high ready position in a single motion. His thumb tensed on the selector switch, ready to click it off safe once the threat was identified. Once his eyes adjusted and he saw it was Dave he lowered the rifle. Dave making eye contact with Mark raised his left hand and threw up an open palm sign to relay the halt signal. Mark released the tension on his selector switch knowing that the even the small sound of it clicking could travel and alert the enemy of their presence.

The movement should not have set him off as it had, but he knew they were deep within enemy territory. However, it had been only a brief time since the last halt that he was not expecting it. Taking a knee to pull security on the small collapsing perimeter Mark waited for the report on the halt. Before there was time to discuss the why, he smelled it.

The smell of a cookfire was in the air. The mixture of burning logs and spiced water were pungent in their nostrils. While the scent would be nominal on a normal day after patrolling, being in the dark for three days straight their heightened senses picked it up far better than they normally would have done. Without possessing the keen scent abilities of a bloodhound, they were unable to pinpoint the exact location of the camp.

However, after doing so many of these missions in the past they would estimate that they were within 200 meters of the perimeter. Potentially, they were closer depending on how heavy or sparse the vegetation was growing near and around the camp. Fortunately, they did know that it was to the East based on wind direction. It was time to establish their objective rally point and begin planning for their reconnaissance of the camp over the next two days.

Slowly the men collapsed their halt into a tighter perimeter to discuss the recon rotation and rest cycle. The men reapplied camouflage to both their skin and to the ghillie suits they wore. Mark, not forgetting the touch up the spot on his face pulled out the camo-stick and quickly reapplied. As the team rotated between pulling security detail, the others drank water, checked weapons and ammunition, and quickly devoured some jerky. Mark worked out a recon rotation that would start once everyone was able to get some rest and prepare their equipment load outs.

They took caution to make little noise this close to the camp as any sound could be fatal. Mark positioned himself facing north next to a fallen log that provided a good amount of concealment and overwatch. The cover it provided was minimal as bullets from the AK-47's would likely rip right through the rotten trunk.

The few hours of rest passed quickly as Kris and Ben moved to start their recon. Mark maintained his position as Dave and Pete adjusted and collapsed the perimeter as the pair started to move east. Kris and Ben had not moved ten feet when Mark heard something thud against the log that he was next to. Instinctively looking down he found in the dim night light the outline of a...

"GRENADE!" Mark shouted.

He was not sure if Kris and Ben were able to take cover in time as he attempted to get as small as possible behind the log. The blast had deafened him, and he felt a searing pain in his side. Dazed, he rolled back into the perimeter and was quickly pulled into a patch of grass by Dave as he tried to stand up.

Dave simply pointed in the direction of darkness where Mark was able to see muzzle flashes throughout the jungle foliage. Slowly coming out of the daze Mark began to return fire. Unable to hear anything he returned fire in what he believed was the best direction based off the most recent muzzle flashes.

In the midst of the battle Mark swore he heard a scream in the direction Kris and Ben had gone followed by a flash of blue light. *Were the enemy throwing concussion grenades?* Mark thought. *He wondered why he had heard the scream when all he could hear was ringing currently and why the flash was not bigger.*

Mark let the thought go as the muzzle flashes seemed to be getting closer and the team was in dire need to tactically retreat to a more defendable location. The last location they had identified was at least 500 meters back. Since Dave and Pete were the only two nearby Mark passed the signal for rally point and they began to bound back out of the area to regroup. One-by-one they moved in a leapfrog manner engaging only as necessary to not give the enemy their location.

Each time Mark got up to move the pain in his side was like fire, fighting through it was difficult, but his will to survive and fight for his men kept him going. Running he heard another scream. While he did not check back, he noticed a blue glow temporarily light up the area before disappearing. He made his way past Pete who was engaging the enemy. As he crossed a small embankment he fell into a shallow creek before making it past Dave.

Dave moved to grab Mark and helped tuck him behind some cover. He looked over the wounds quickly and stuffed some gauze into his side. Even in the dark Mark could tell there was a grim expression on his face as Pete rushed by to an area past the creek.

"We got to move! They're still com..." Pete yelled in muffled tones as a stray round took him in the head. Mark watched in wonder as Pete's body fell, lifeless, leaving a pale blue after image that screamed clearly and dissolved into small particles floating upward. Mark looked at Dave who seemed to not notice the event as he quickly moved over to Pete and tore off one of his ID tags and stuffed it into his shirt.

"What are you gawkin' at man, we gotta go." Dave garbled out as he shook Mark, still staring at the blank space that had the ghostly image of Pete.

"Yea, man. Did you..." Realizing Dave was unaware of what was happening he knew he must be seeing things from his wounds. "Hey, I saw your face, I'm gone. Get out of here. I'll buy you sometime." Mark ripped off a dog tag and tossed it over to him. He readied two grenades and put his rifle on full auto with a fresh magazine as Dave shook his head changing directions to evade the enemy. Finally looking down at his wound Mark saw it was bleeding steadily despite the bandage which likely ruptured his liver. Slowly standing Mark moved to peak around his cover to see how much time he had before the enemy was upon him.

As he peaked around the cover three Vietcong were standing there walking side-by-side in the shallow creek with a focus on Pete's location. As Mark's head poked out, they immediately shifted focus, but Mark was able to quickly get his rifle up and unload it into all three. As the three fell they all left behind the same blue image that dissolved into small particles that screamed as they faded. He knew he must be losing it now.

Shots rang out from somewhere behind the fallen soldiers hitting Mark in the chest causing him to drop his rifle and fall face first into the creek. Mark tried crawling towards Pete's location but could not make it out of the creek bed before four more soldiers were on him.

"You, turn over!" one of the soldiers commanded. Mark did not comply. He probably could not move even if he tried, so he just slumped his head down on the bank of the creek. The soldier then stated something in Vietnamese to the others and they moved over to Mark. "You come with us now!

The soldiers grabbed Mark by the arms as he grunted in pain. Lifting him up and turning him around to face the one in charge. "No Charlie, we're goin' to Hell." Mark released the spoons on his two grenades he had removed the pins from as he waited for them to walk up to him. The soldiers tried to run in the precious seconds before the explosions but were unable to escape their demise. Time seemed to slow for Mark as the explosion unfolded.

He knew he would die almost instantly, but he was able to watch the explosion take each of the soldiers in turn and their individual forms scream and dissipate as they ceased to exist. The blast had no effect on Mark as the initial grenade that had deafened him had. He clearly heard the blast of the grenades, the crack of bones and trees, the screams of the soldiers. In fact, his hearing was back to normal instead of the intense ringing it had been since he was wounded.

Looking around, he saw his own lifeless body on the ground torn to pieces and yet he was standing. Gazing at his hands he was not blue like the others but had a yellowish almost golden hue to his skin. He also realized that it was now daytime, and a horn was blowing from off in the distance.

Trying to determine which direction the horn was sounding from, a large, winged woman flew down through the canopy, scooped Mark up, and rose out of the jungle in seconds. The sky was illuminated in a golden hue that was now supporting a massive fortress in the clouds. In the arms of the woman Mark rapidly ascended towards the fortress and was gently placed onto a terrace with many other golden-hued people adorned in warrior armor from various historical eras.

"What is this?" Mark asks.

A man stepped forward looking like he belonged in a Viking raiding party. "An invitation."

"An invitation? For what exactly?"

"The Eternal Battle, of course."

"Wait. Like as in Heaven and Hell?"

"Yes, and yet, also no. Heaven and Hell, Chaos and Order, Light and Dark, Valhalla and Niflheim, God and Satan, Good and Evil. It's all about balance and each need warriors. You have demonstrated that there is more than just completing the mission. The capability to make complex decisions and lead in stressful situations, taking others welfare above your own personal safety, and facing the enemy despite insurmountable odds. He makes it back, by the way."

"Wait, who makes it back?"

"Dave, I figured you would like to have known."

"That is good to know. He only had three more weeks before his tour was over. So, you're saying it doesn't matter that I'm not religious?"

"Of course not. Had anyone that you saw die chose this path you had seen them leave golden or worse turn red. We all have a choice. Only most choose to spend eternity in bliss. It is up to us to keep and maintain the balance. While you saw them die and dissolve in an instant, they were all given this decision and some take days to decide, but most choose eternal bliss over responsibility. And even some choose the opposite. While unfortunate it does happen."

"Is that why I don't see Ben or Pete or Kris?"

"The very reason. However, you likely would not see them here regardless if they did stay as they would have been here for days already training and you would meet them there. Time operates differently here."

"Then who are all of these people."

"These are some of our proven warriors. You may talk with them to make your decision, if you wish."

"How long do I have to decide?"

"As long as you need."

Taking it all in, Mark paced around the terrace while the warriors watched him in stoic silence. Stopping at the edge of the terrace, Mark looked down onto the earth below him and to the skies above. Pondering, he wondered what bliss would be like? What will the fighting be like if he chose to stay? Only moments passed as he turned and walked back to the group of warriors.

"I think I've made a decision." A soft groan came from some of the warriors in the group as others shuffled uneasily.

"You have decided so quickly. Are you sure you would not like to dwell on it longer?" the Viking dressed man asked smiling. "Do you not wish to know more about what it means to serve? Or want a description of bliss beyond?"

"No, thank you. You see, I think living an eternity in bliss would be amazing."

Obviously disappointed the man lowers his head. "If this is your de..."

"But I've never wanted to have someone do the work for me. After already serving in the Hell, I've been trudging through, I'd be honored to join your ranks and serve alongside you all." Mark stated as the warriors erupted in a fanfare of cheers.

The pain was searing through the stump of where his lower left arm used to be as Private Lan frantically attempted to put a bandage on his wound. The three other soldiers, including his commander, were dead lying in heaps of smoldering flesh with masks of anguish painted on their faces. The jungle was now silent after the blast.

Scanning the bodies for something to tie off his wound Private Lan could have sworn he saw a golden light fade from the American. Half of his face was now missing and from what remained it was turned upward in a permanent grim smile as it finally stopped twitching. Despite the horridness of his fellow soldiers' bodies and their lifeless expressions Lan felt the American's face would be the image that haunted his dreams for many nights to come.

1:4:5:6:10:12-VI:VIII:XI-A:E:F:G:H:I:J:K

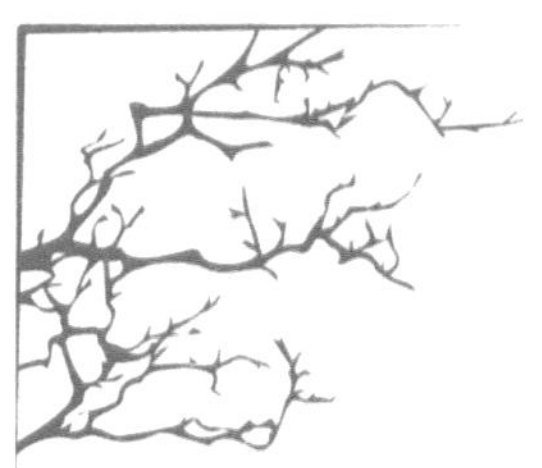

A Last Act

"We're almost home. About twenty minutes out. Yes, I'm driving carefully. Love you too. Bye." Tara said in her typical sing-song voice as she hung up the phone with her husband.

It was a long day at work, but she had finally finished. Had she not been on her way home to start her long-awaited vacation she was sure she would be pulling her hair out. She had picked up her daughters from daycare later than she wanted due to staying at work an hour longer to make sure no one would call her over the break. It would not have been much of a concern on a normal day, but now she was having to deal with the heavy snowfall.

The back roads had begun to be covered but fortunately most people had already made it home by now. The roads were empty save the occasional car coming in the opposite direction heading towards town. The sun had already set, and the darkness and snowfall began making it difficult to see. Tara was determined to get home as she was just as exhausted as her three-year-old and one-year-old, who were fast asleep in the back seat.

The snow started coming down more heavily and the use of high beams did nothing but illuminate more snow than road. Tara slowed her speed to accommodate a safer pace but found herself beginning to slide. Unsure of what her speed was, she knew it was above the safe limit before she started to slow in time.

She applied the brake which only worked for a moment as she started to drift sideways. She tried to correct her steering as the car began to spin, losing control of the vehicle in the slickness of the road. Her urgency to get home had caused her to lapse in good judgement and she was attempting drastically to correct that decision.

No longer able to get control of the vehicle she suddenly felt herself jerk upward out of her seat as the car left the road and began to flip. Screams filled the air as the world tumbled over and over outside as the windows began to shatter.

The car flipped endlessly as toys and trash and snow flew through the interior of the cabin. When it seemed they would never stop the car slammed abruptly to a halt. The force caused Tara to hit the side of her head. The blow came swift and sudden. There was no pain as she was rendered immediately unconscious.

The sound of her children crying woke Tara up. She found herself on the ground outside the car lying on her back in a bank of snow. She was banged up, her head pounding, her arms cut up, her vision foggy. More screams and crying from her children forced her to focus.

She noticed that she was thrown out of the passenger side of the car as the door was hanging open. The vehicle rested on the roof and the driver's side door was pinned up against an electric pole now bent by the force of the crash, the top of it exploded in sparks every couple seconds.

With agonizing pain shooting up her legs and back, she stood up and moved over to the back door and opened it. Her oldest daughter with eyes tightly shut cried out to her, "Mommy! Help!" As her youngest simply wailed in fear.

Working the safety belt on her youngest daughter took effort with it being upside down. She finally got her daughter down and placed her on a blanket that had fallen on the roof as she began to help her oldest. "Mommy! Help!" She yelled again, reaching out for assistance toward her.

"I'm here baby. I got you." Tara tried to say in a calm voice. As she was working the latch on the belt the smell of gas wafted into her nostrils. Panic began to set in immediately and she pulled harder on the straps to get her out of the seat.

Her hands fumbled at the latch in a futile effort as they felt numb and difficult to manipulate. After many failed attempts, the buckle snapped open, and her daughter fell into her arms free of the restraint. "Mommy! Help!" Her daughter exclaimed again arms stretched out.

"Yes baby, I have you." Tara picked up her other daughter and the blanket and wrapped them both in it. As she moved away from the vehicle sparks began falling from the pole as fragments of the wire frayed apart and ignited the gas. The flames spread quickly over the bottom of the car and spread to the ground around the hood of the car igniting the gas in the snow. The front of the vehicle now surrounded in flames silhouetting the two tiny figures Tara carried in her arms as she made her way to safety with her daughters.

Sitting near a mailbox Tara held her oldest in front of her as she held onto her sister. Holding them both tightly wrapped in the blanket they watched as the car started to become further engulfed in flames. Sirens began to be heard in the distance as someone could be heard running up the snow-covered driveway behind them.

"I love you girls. Help is coming. You're going to be fine." Tara hugged her girls trying to console them and calm them down. Their crying persisted regardless. She held them close as the fire began to grow larger casting them in a warm glow. A man rounded the edge of his driveway and ran onto the road.

"Girls! Are you okay? Were you inside that car? How did you get out?" The man said as he knelt down to examine the two small children wrapped in a blanket.

"Mommy! Help!" was all Tara discerned as her oldest daughter gestured towards the car where the man knelt beside her girls. Tara's breathing grew shallow and labored from the smoke. She sensed her head bleeding and observed the pool of blood beneath her expanding. Uncertain of her surroundings, she experienced every sensation as if it were her own despite being trapped in her seat. Her daughters' survival became her sole focus. She could only gaze intently at them as flames and smoke enveloped her vision. The sound of approaching sirens diminished quickly from her ears despite the proximity as calmly melded into eternity.

11-XI-B:D

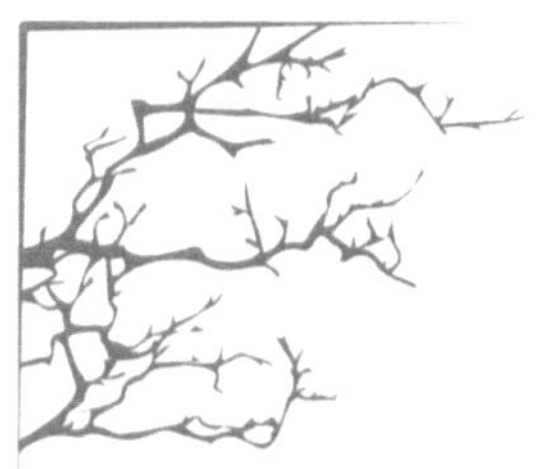

Gloom

Dillon had been enjoying his summer camp experience with the scouts. His troop was busy earning merit badges all week, cooking meals by campfire, exploring the wilderness, and his favorite part, swimming every day. After working on various badges for the day and getting camp ready for the evening meal, Dillon and his troop always went to the pool for an hour to swim.

On the pool's final day of camp, it was swarming with kids from different scout troops. Dillon and his pals endeavored to secure a portion of the pool for themselves to enjoy. They engaged in various water games such as "Marco Polo" and water tag and held competitions to see who could produce the biggest splash or execute the funniest dive or jump. Currently, they were engaged in a breath-holding competition. The boys submerged themselves, attempting to disregard their friends' attempts to make them laugh or pull faces to coax them into exhaling prematurely and resurfacing.

The boys had been enjoying this game for several rounds when the whistle blew for a 10-minute warning to swap out. Agreeing to one more game everyone took their breath and went under as more kids were coming in and taking up positions around the pool for their time. The game continued like the previous games as one-by-one of Dillon's friends gave up to some trick being played or having to go up for air.

Dillon was one of three of his buddies left when he tried to get either of them to laugh by pretending to sing like an opera singer. Dillon ended up blowing out too much of his own air laughing at himself and started for the surface straining to get new air into his lungs.

As he was about to break the surface a dark mass appeared above him. Dillon heard the crash of water above him and felt something collide with him as the remaining air left his lungs. Dillon frantically tried to reach the surface but was entangled with the mass that had fallen on him. He felt his arms being grabbed and instinctively pulled away trying to get to the surface.

Surrounded by the chaos Dillon could no longer hold his breath. Gripped with fear his body forced him to take a breath. The water rushed into his lungs and as panicked as he was a sense of serene calm suddenly washed over him as his vision began to fade and his body fell limp. The darkness quickly swallowed the sun filled day.

Dillon felt weightless in the darkness. It was cold and void of sound. He could sense in the darkness around him as if there were others nearby but unable to see anyone or anything beyond his outstretched hand. Fear began to grip Dillon in the cold darkness as he began to wonder if what he was feeling was himself drowning in the pool. Starting to panic Dillon twisted and turned his weightless body searching for anywhere to go.

He tried to cry out for his parents, his friends, and even God when the darkness was instantly torn away by a bright golden light that now enveloped his vision. The light was bright, yet not blinding, warm, and inviting, and he thought he heard music emanating from all directions. Though unfamiliar with the music, it sounded strangely familiar.

Upon the appearance of the light, Dillon experienced a peaceful sensation washing over him, causing him to cease his struggle as all fear and doubt vanished. These emotions were replaced by joy and a profound sense of peace, an indescribable feeling he desired to endure indefinitely due to its deep impact on him.

In the rush of the changing environment Dillon had not realized that he was now on firm ground. There was no visible floor beneath his feet, yet he knew that whatever he stood on was solid. Unsure of where he needed to go, he began walking in no particular direction. Despite it being a random direction, it felt like it was the right decision as the music became more vivid and the warmth of the light became more inviting.

Dillon walked intently and though he had walked for a long time he did not feel fatigued. In the distance he saw something reflecting the light around him. With a goal in sight, he began to run. Just as he started, he felt something slam into his chest and push him backwards. Before he could steady himself and figure out what it was or where it came from, another force hit his chest. Then another and another knocking him backwards. The relentless blows soon knocked him to the ground onto his back.

He found he could not scream out as the force hitting his chest took the breath from his lungs. The sound of the music began to fade, replaced by rushing water. The warm welcoming light was replaced by a piercing radiance that made him shut his eyes tight. A wave of inaudible voices came from every direction as the blows to his chest continued. Finally, breath filled his lungs, and he was able to roll over to his side as he coughed up water onto the concrete pad surrounding the pool.

The sun above made him squint from its penetrating light. Cheers and claps from the scouts that had gathered around filled his ears. A lifeguard urged him to take it slow and remain lying down as he continued to check his vital signs. Dillon looked around in a haze and found his friends close by who apparently had gone and found their scoutmaster, but nowhere did he see the warm inviting light. No longer did he hear the familiar unknown music, and he certainly felt like he had run several miles as fatigue washed over him.

The lifeguard began explaining that Dillon had another scout fall on him as he was coming up for air. The other scouts waiting to get in the pool decided to throw one of their buddies in before the start of their time and did not see Dillon underwater. He continued by saying that he had performed CPR for over three minutes. The lifeguard told him he was incredibly lucky and that someone up above was looking out for him.

Dillon continued to let the lifeguard do his duties and responded when needed, but his mind was elsewhere. It seemed like he was gone much longer than three minutes. He now felt like something was missing that he never knew he had. That indescribable feeling of warmth, joy, and peace he felt for only a fleeting moment was gone. It made him feel as if there were now a void within himself despite being thankful for being alive. A void that he wished he could somehow fill again.

It had been years since Dillon had his brush with death, but it was often on his mind. He did not think much about the actual drowning, but more about the experience he went through as he was drowning. Since the incident he had felt the void within him grow and he found himself becoming more depressed and less outgoing than he used to be.

He still hung out with friends, played and wrote music, and worked on his bachelor's degree to help him fill the void left by the experience. He ran through the machinations of life to keep himself busy, trying not to focus on the feeling the void left behind in an attempt to recreate the feeling of joy and peace he experienced. Unfortunately, the only one thing that ever brought him closer to that experience had been drugs.

Dillon began experimenting with drugs when he first got to college and found that the feeling, he received from the various drugs he tried simulated the experience he had when he was younger. Under the influence he felt the warmth, he heard the music, he experienced the joy, the peace, the calm.

The only difference is that the experiences were singular in effect. He could never recreate more than two of the effects and never came close to the actual event again. However, this did not stop his experimentation. Unfortunately, he always ended his experience disappointed and needing to try something else, something more, something different in an attempt to fill the void.

Dillon had a plan to combine all the experiences, but never wanted to try it as he was likely to kill himself trying it. He was always willing to try something as long it did not kill him because he still cared about finishing school, spending time with his friends and his girlfriend. The thought of ending it all never crossed his mind even with his depression always nagging at him.

However, he was now in a low point of his life as the drugs and alcohol had driven his grades down and he was losing his scholarships. He had recently lost his job from not showing up. His girlfriend was cheating on him with his best friend and his life in general was now beginning to spiral out of his control. Due to this low point, he felt it was finally time to try his plan as life could not appear to be any worse than its current state.

Preparing a screwdriver, his favorite drink, he also gathered his collection of pills he planned on taking to have his experience. Prepping everything in the living room he turned on some music and cranked it up since he no longer had his friend as a roommate.

Dillon took a seat on the couch and shoved a handful of pills into his mouth, washing them down with his screwdriver. He sank back into the cushions and closed his eyes listening to the music and waited for the pills to take effect.

It did not take long for something to happen; the initial feeling was warmth that started in his head and moved down his body. Despite the room's low light, it felt as if he were sunbathing on a beach as his body warmed up. He smiled as his body began to go numb and feel weightless though he knew he was still sitting on the couch.

He felt as if he were aware of everything in the room, the smells, the sounds of the music, the feel of the couch surrounding him and floor beneath his feet. The taste of his drink was still on his tongue thirsty for another as he reached for the table. He blindly found it taking another swallow as his head swayed from the influence of the drugs and alcohol.

He anxiously awaited more sitting in his solitude. Dillon could not tell if the next sensation was within his mind or through his eyelids as it seemed the room suddenly brightened to accompany the warmth that his body was already experiencing.

He did not dare open his eyes in fear of losing the experience but also from fear of being blinded by the brilliance. He kept his eyes shut, continuing to embrace the experience in pure enjoyment.

Dillon was enjoying the warmth, the numb weightlessness, and brilliance, but was becoming impatient with how long it was taking to move onto the next experience. Frustrated he grabbed another handful of pills from the table and finished the rest of his screwdriver. Upon sitting back his body immediately began feeling an overwhelming calm. Tears filled his eyes as he accomplished combining all the feelings he had once experienced so many years ago drowning in that pool.

He felt as if he were now floating and no longer planted in his couch. The warmth and brilliance encompassed him. He peacefully took it all in as the music reverberated in his ears as a dull roar nothing like the music he once heard. Yet, it was enough to satisfy the experience he had been searching for these past years.

Lost in time he floated in his mind taking in his bliss. He dreamed of walking down that lighted floorless path again. Hearing that familiar unknown music that came from everywhere. The explosion of light behind his eyelids, the warmth his body felt. The music playing from the stereo paled in its comparison and he started to become distraught by his own illusion. The feeling of bliss in his own reality was tearing him down, regardless of how close it was to his previous experience. It taunted him knowing it would end eventually.

Turning his thoughts back to his bliss he felt as if he was beginning to come down as he was starting to lose his warmth. He was unaware of how much time had been spent on his euphoria, but he knew he did not want it to end just yet. He blindly reached forward to the table once again to grab for more pills and his drink. He could not find them. Reaching down he found that the table was no longer in front of him, and the couch was no longer present beneath him.

He opened his eyes and in an instant the warmth, the brilliance, the music, the weightlessness...the calm; were gone. He was back in the familiar and vast darkness that he dwelled within before his grand experience before.

Dillon tried to yell but was unable to produce any noise in the void. Looking around he realized why the weightlessness was gone. He was unable to feel his feet, yet he stood on a barren slab of rock that seemed to be floating within the abyssal dark surrounding him. Only able to see an arm's length in front of himself he could not tell how large or small it might be.

Dillon had read about purgatory, but he never thought that he would end up there. The darkness lifted in the nearby area as if lit by a sliver of moonlight. It illuminated a massive stone gateway with pale white wooden carved doors. Among the carvings were effigies of chained souls and hooded skeletal masters leading the souls off into the distance. A giant pair of judgement scales carved into the top were split by the door's center.

Soon a cloaked being whose form was of gray swirling smoke oozed out of the center crack of the doors and came to rest in front of him. It coalesced into the form of a sludge-dripping skeleton. The grotesque figure donned in a black gaseous cloak asked him to account for his life's actions. Dillon tried to explain himself, but he was consumed by feelings of guilt and shame.

He felt like he had wasted his life and had let down everyone who had ever cared for him simply because he had only tried to find that feeling again. He pleaded for mercy as the cloaked figure floated in the abyss in silent judgement. He pleaded until his voice was so hoarse, that he could no longer speak without the words tearing at his throat and still it watched.

The being raised its arm towards Dillon extending dripping fingers toward his face. "You have been judged." It spoke in a cold raspy voice as tendrils of smoke from the cloak began to surround Dillon's neck. "This is your fate as you have decided, and your punishment follows." Dillon opened his mouth to let out a scream as the tendrils tightened around his neck.

As soon as he began to shout the sludge covered hand plunged into his mouth as the being began to dissolve and go down his throat choking him. The taste of oil and putridness filled his mouth and the sensation of both hot vomit and chilled water began to fill his mouth and throat. He could not breathe and felt as if he were going to be sick but had no room to do so.

His eyes began to water as his need to breathe was becoming increasingly desperate. There seemed to be no end to this torture as his need for breath and the feeling of nausea were becoming unbearable. The being continued to pour his essence into Dillon as darkness closed in around him and he lost consciousness.

"Keep it up Dillon, the ambulance is on the way." Is all he heard as more vomit spewed from his mouth and onto the floor of his apartment. Barely able to open his eyes, all he could see was a massive pile of vomit on the floor below him littered with pills as he lay face down on the couch.

His former best friend was knelt next to him screaming into the phone for the medical team to hurry up. Dillon wondered why he was there and if he had seen the demon that was torturing him. The horrible flavor in his mouth and the vomiting had his body feeling like it had been hit by a truck. The worst feeling by far was the sense of dread that if he died there was no longer a peaceful place waiting for him, but that cold darkness and torture with more of those dark entities.

Seven years had passed since Dillon had been judged, but he could still feel the tendrils around his neck and the taste of its essence as if it were still happening. He had persistent nightmares that kept him awake most nights until exhaustion. His depression had only increased since the event and he now lived with a lot of anxiety due to the experience. He refused to take anymore drugs or even contemplate suicide ever again for fear of that place. The best he managed was to work as much as possible to distract himself from his misery for as long as possible.

Dillon ended up getting a job at a gas station that was open all night. It was located only a block from his apartment so he would always stop by when he needed something. His boss liked him because he was reliable and would come in when needed, but Dillon only came to take his mind off his horrors.

The other cashiers liked him because he would take an unwanted shift or cover for them when they had to go to an appointment or anything else during their shifts, making the work environment great for everyone. Dillon once again did not mind the break in his own routine, because it took his mind off that cold dark void embedded into his soul.

He preferred to work most nights as sleeping in the day helped with the dreams. Due to living so close and the gas station having a kitchen he would also tend to show up early to get something to eat before his shift. Tonight, was no different as Dillon was not supposed to start his shift for another hour. He had already gotten ready for work and his mind had begun going to dark places. Since it was a night shift, he decided it would be better to get to work earlier. At least he would have someone to talk to until they got off shift before customers stopped coming in for the night. It always got progressively more boring doing inventory when no one else was around.

Tina was on the counter tonight as Dillon walked in and gave him a warm smile as she checked out a customer. The fairly large establishment only had a few people wandering around the aisles at the moment and only three vehicles at the pumps. The night had already started to slow down. "Would you like the usual Dillon?" Tina asked pointing to the cigarette display as Dillon was walking towards the soda cabinet.

"Yea, thanks. I'll be there in a minute." Dillon navigated the store to grab a soda and a burrito then made his way up to the register to buy it along with the cigarettes Tina set aside for him. As he waited his turn in line, his mind could not help but drift yet again to the darkness. The void always creeped up on him when he did not keep himself preoccupied enough and standing in line was one of the many activities that seemed to lure him back into its dark depths.

Dillon snapped out of his train of thought by Tina calling him up to the counter. As his items were being rung up someone came in and stopped her from finishing. He realized that the person behind him had a gun pointed towards Tina. He was commanded to get out of the way as a man in a ski mask yelled at Tina to empty the cash register.

Dillon stepped to the side with his arms raised as the man demanded, getting a glimpse of someone at the pumps getting on their phone as he was pushed into a rack of potato chips and fell to the ground. As the scene unfolded police showed up outside within minutes before the thief could get his cash and leave. Reacting, the thief took cover behind some shelves as the police began to negotiate with him.

The thief became more frustrated arguing with the police and paced the aisle. Tina moved thinking he was distracted enough to get to cover, and he turned to shoot her as Dillon stood to intercept him and ended up getting shot himself. The police opened fire through the glass doors and shot the thief several times as he fell knocking many items off the shelves around him.

The officers rushed to the scene and ensured the thief was down, calling an ambulance for Dillon, but also to provide aid for the thief. Tina grabbed several rags for Dillon to put on his wound for the bleeding. Dillon looked over at the thief who was sitting up, becoming surrounded by a growing darkness with a wide-eyed expression on his face.

The sound of ethereal screams came from within the darkness as dark skeletal forms erupted from the void surrounding the thief. The boney hands tore into his flesh and latched onto him. He screamed as they pulled him into the dark void. The screams of tortured souls and his own blood curdling wail echoed into silence as the dark veil dissipated revealing two officers leaning over his bloodied corpse attempting to provide aid.

An officer had Dillon lie on his back as his bleeding was not slowing down. He feared he was soon to meet the same fate as the thief and hoped the officer could help him. Dillon cried as he started to lose his vision. Overcome by the blood loss and the situation his body started to convulse.

Tina screamed his name and the sound of the officer talking to him waned as darkness surrounded him. The sound was replaced by what sounded like clawing skeletal hands coming toward him. He did not want to open his eyes knowing what he would see reaching for him but decided to meet his fate head on no longer living and now dying in fear.

He opened his eyes surrounded by the familiar brilliant warm glow. Embraced by the warmth that he was wrapped in all those years ago when he almost drowned. The light engulfed him as the overwhelming peace of the music returned as well soothing the dread and worries that had been burdening him for decades. Absorbing the joy in it all he began to dissolve into light, becoming a part of it himself as his former world around him faded into the brilliance of the light.

1:6:8-G:H:I:J:K

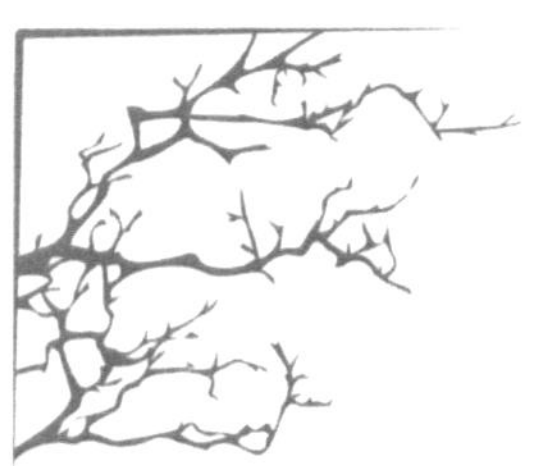

For Him

Valerie was overjoyed to be the guest of honor at the ceremony. Drake had told her that she was special, and she knew that of course. They had been dating for a couple of years now and he told her that he would make tonight memorable for her. She was used to getting what she wanted as well as being worshipped wherever she went, but tonight was turning out to be so much more.

Tonight, was seemingly no different as everyone here bent to her every beck and call with whatever she needed. It was strange due to all of the people doing the serving and taking her orders were friends of her parents and people she had known most of her life. The normal wait staff must have had the night off, but as the night went on it became more natural. It was her birthday after all, and Drake did promise that it would be memorable, so she should be the center of attention in spite of what everyone thought.

She flowed from guest to guest in her white gown that her mother had picked out for her for the evening. She talked, dined, and visited for hours with friends, family, and the occasional stranger, who oddly enough asked her to leave the party, more than once, with them. Had she not been in a relationship with Drake she may have taken a couple of them up on the offer as they did look rather handsome.

While they were rather convincing, she was in a relationship, and she was not about to ruin what she had with Drake. She had lost track of time having drinks on the terrace with some friends of the family under the full moonlight as the clock struck midnight. She was escorted in by her friends as her parents called for her to come up to the front of the room where they were standing with Drake.

"Valerie." Her father started. "We celebrate you this evening and the coming of a new life. Drake has told us so much about his time with you. We all wanted to share in this magical moment. It is time for everyone to don your masks."

Looking around Valerie watched as her friends and family put on a mask that resembled various horned devilish creatures that were grey in color almost like stone. Everyone began forming a circle around the four of them. Everywhere she looked all she could see were the masked faces of people she should know, but no longer able to identify them.

Within the crowd she saw only a few faces. None of them she recognized as friends or family, but as the strangers from the party that had asked her to leave earlier. They just stared at her intently as chanting began from everyone that was masked. The strangers seemed to wear a look of sadness on their faces for some reason.

"Praise be to her. Praise be to him." Echoed throughout the room in a soft murmur.

"Valerie, I know this must be confusing, but we are symbols of the unchanging, while you and Drake are the ones to be celebrated. He has told us how much you care for each other, and we want to see that last forever." Her father spoke loudly for all to hear stepping behind Drake as her mother stepped behind her. "So, we ask of thee, do you love him."

"Yes." She had no idea why her father was so accepting of the relationship let alone going to this length to marry them. He had only spent a little time with Drake of which she was aware. Strangely, she was overcome with joy as she looked at Drake standing in front of her smiling.

"Do you give yourself to him completely?"

"Yes." She was nearly in tears holding back her happiness.

"Should the need arise, would you die for him?"

With a slight hesitation she paused and thought...*oh 'in sickness and in health until death do us part',* "Yes." *What an odd way to say it.*

She smiled and looked at Drake who was looking intently at her. Holding his hand, he felt so calm. She was sure he could feel her hands sweating from the impromptu ceremony. Her father continued to speak, but she no longer had to answer so she focused on Drake until he looked away and began to answer the questions as well.

"Drake, do you love him?"

"Yes." He stated with joy in his voice.

Wait, did he say 'Him?' Valerie thought. *I must have been mistaken that can't be right I was too focused on looking at Drake.*

"Do you give yourself to Him completely?"

"Yes." He said again as his smile widened.

Valerie began to look concerned. *I know for a fact he said 'Him' that time. What is going on?*

"And should the need arise, would you die for Him?"

"Yes."

"Wait, what is going on? Who are you talking about?" Valerie shouted as her mother grabbed her by the arms from behind.

"Shh. Just listen dear. All will be revealed."

"The willingness of the two has been attested and the flock has borne witness. We ask of thee does the need arise?"

The house started to rumble as the people in the crowd began to raise their arms in praise. Valerie tried to run but her mother continued to hold her arms and Drake held her hands tight as he looked at her smiling. Looking around no one seemed to care about the rumbling as the chanting had simply become "Praise to Him." As quickly as the rumbling began it vanished. Regaining her wits Valerie saw one of the masked guests moving forward. They stopped in front of Valerie and Drake. The man under the mask remained motionless as the demonic face began to shift and talk as if it were alive.

"I am pleased by your willingness. My bride and I look forward to walking the Earth once again. The need does arise."

Shocked, Valerie watched as the mask formed back into a simple grey mask and the person within moved back amongst the guests. The unmasked strangers with heads bowed began to turn away. As their backs were turned Valerie swore she could see translucent white wisps resembling wings beginning to sprout from their backs as they made their way towards the exit. A wreath of light shown around their heads made it easy to keep sight of them in the sea of people, but she eventually lost them as the light faded into the darkness of the room behind them. Losing sight of them in the crowd of people, she turned back to her family.

As she was about to ask Drake what was going on she watched in horror as her father sliced open his throat in front of her. His blood splattering her in the face as his throat was sliced open. She tried to reach up to hold his throat, but he held onto her hands with a tight grip.

Looking down at his hands she saw a ceremonial blade at her own throat that her mother held at her own neck. She felt it slice effortlessly into her flesh and sever her arteries and open her windpipe as the blood began to pour out of her as she started to suffocate and bleed out at the same time.

Drake began to lead her to the ground, somehow still smiling. She looked around at the crowd, the masked faces still chanting, but the sounds faded as the blood rushed out of her. Thinking back on the strangers Valerie knew that they somehow tried to get her out of this situation and failed. She was too blind to see through the signs throughout the years that her family was part of a cult. She had just thought she was special and was being treated as such.

As her vision darkened, she blinked and in an instant she was standing over her body with Drake by her side. The two of them, shocked, embraced in the darkness. They watched as their wounds healed and their bodies rose. It was as if they were looking through a window of the scene they had just recently left. The people on the other side fell to their knees in worship of the two that rose from death. Valerie and Drake could not hear the people, but their former selves, the entities with solid black eyes and voices that rang with layers of sounds as they spoke, they heard clearly.

"You are unworthy."

The two former embodiments of Valerie and Drake began to massacre guests from the party. They set the cultists on fire, crushed them with an invisible force, physically ripped them apart, and other unspeakable horrors. They relished the violence and chaos. Delighted in the blood that now blanketed their flesh.

Valerie and Drake watched in horror from their solitary viewing location. Very few of the cultists ran. Most remained in prostrated bows as they were torn to pieces. Valerie's parents stood and smiled as they watched the carnage. The two entities ended their feast by each reaching into one of her parents' chests and ripping their hearts out to devour them. When the two entities were finished, they turned in the direction of Valerie and Drake's awaiting souls and smiled.

"That was just the beginning of your torment" The entity wearing Valerie's skin said as she snapped her fingers. The darkness surrounding Valerie and Drake began to fill with moans and screeches from all directions. Sounds of skittering and wet slaps echoed in the darkness. Claws tore into unseen walls scraping louder and louder as whatever horrors it belonged to drew themselves closer. Valerie and Drake screamed as unseen figures lurched from the darkness and clawed, grasped, and tore at them, dragging them deep into the abyssal void.

1:3:4:6:7:8:9:10:12-VIII:XI-B:F:G:H:I:J:K

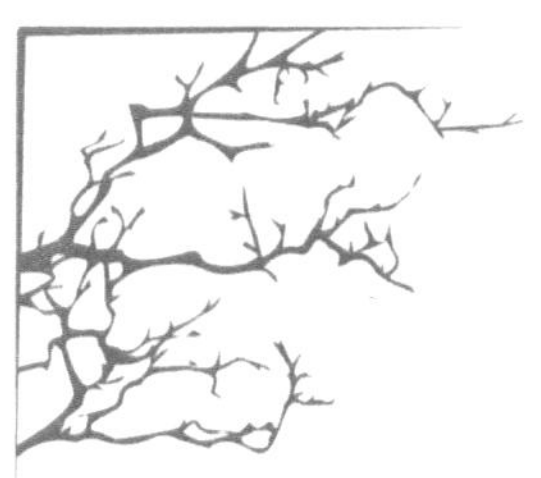

Déjà Vu

Leaving the office after another average day of work meant Pete would take his normal route down the back roads to avoid all the evening traffic. While it may take ten or fifteen extra minutes, he enjoyed the scenery it provided. It was fall and the leaves were starting to change so the drive was more enjoyable this time of the year.

He passed Miss Johnson checking her mail like clockwork, which meant he was about twenty minutes from his house. He watched her disappear in his rearview mirror as he continued down the winding county road. Taking in the view he pulled up his music app on his phone and started to play some Johnny Cash to finish out his ride.

He placed his phone down as "Fulsom Prison Blues" began playing taking his eyes off the road for a second to find the spot to place it. As he put it down, he hit a pothole in the road he failed to see when his eyes were diverted, the jolt surprised him and caused him to jerk the wheel.

Gripping the steering wheel, he tried to regain control and straighten out the car as a startled deer jumped out in front of his vehicle. Yanking the wheel to the right he swerved hard to avoid hitting it and caused him to overcorrect the car. He clipped the guard rail with the back end of his car causing it to start flipping.

The world became a blur as his vision tried to focus on the rapidly rotating horizon. Objects within the car tumbled into the air and became suspended from the force of the rotation. His phone flew out of the space he placed it in almost immediately and hit him in the head before he lost sight of it.

Mere seconds went by in slow motion as the glass shattered from his windows. An explosion of white clouded his vision as the air bag erupted in his face throwing his arms off the steering wheel. Sharp pain immediately followed in his left arm as he felt his shoulder pop and tear. A few seconds more of chaos and the vehicle came to a stop resting upside down.

Helplessly hanging upside down, he felt around with his right arm trying for the seatbelt with no success. His head was pinned by the steering wheel and forced to face out the window. Now able to focus, he saw that his left arm had been ripped off and was bleeding heavily. He knew he would bleed out soon if no help arrived and knowing this road, it was not likely this time of day.

He struggled as best he could but was pinned by something, unable to budge an inch in his awkward and injured position. He tried searching for his phone but was unable to find it blindly reaching out with his hand. The vision in his eyes began to fade as he was losing consciousness from the blood loss as a deer slowly sauntered by. It's hooves scraped the asphalt as it made its way to the other side of the road. Pete's vision faded away as did his hearing as he lost consciousness...

<<<<<<

...Pete would take his normal route down the back roads to avoid all the evening traffic. While it may take ten or fifteen extra minutes, he enjoyed the scenery it provided. It was fall and the leaves were starting to change so the drive was even more enjoyable this time of the year.

He passed Miss Johnson checking her mail like clockwork which meant he was about twenty minutes from his house. He watched her disappear in his rearview mirror as he continued down the winding county road. Taking in the view he grabbed his phone to open up his music app as a feeling of Déjà Vu washed over him. As he thought about the Déjà Vu he swerved to avoid hitting a pothole near the center of the road. It had not been fixed in months despite other sections of this same road being repaved closer to town.

Putting down his phone, Pete turned on the radio to be greeted by an ad for yet another mattress store sale. Always on sale and always going out of business it seemed, but never actually happening and prices never actually dropping. He chuckled to himself as he passed a deer standing on the side of the road opposite of his that simply stood and watched as he passed. As he rounded the curve, he realized the feeling of Déjà Vu had passed. As quickly as it came it was gone.

>>>>>>

Taking a break from the office Pete decided it was time to get some lunch at his favorite deli. He hated the hustle and bustle of the streets at this time, but the deli was only a couple of blocks from the office and well worth the walk. The crowd was quite boisterous today and everyone was in a hurry to get wherever they had to be. He had already been forcefully bumped into by multiple people who were obviously more important than he was and off to something way more important than what he was doing.

Only in one of those instances it turned out one of the guys that did it was simply trying to get to an empty street bench to smoke a cigarette. It would have only taken another 5 seconds at the speed they were walking, but who was he to judge? Pete brushed it off as he did not care for the confrontation, and it would accomplish nothing except cut into his own lunch time.

He continued the short walk and stood in horror across the street from where his favorite deli was supposed to be. The front of the tall building had the first several floors obscured with covered scaffolding. The building was evidently getting a makeover of some sort. Pete's heart sank and he wondered what he would do now for something to eat.

As he was looking up and down the street for other options, he noticed that the ends of the scaffolding were opened up and that foot traffic was still allowed in front of the building. As if by willing it into existence, someone exited the scaffolding exit across from him with an order from the deli in their hand indicating that the deli was indeed open.

Pulling out his phone to check the time he dropped some change. He felt he still had plenty of time. He rushed to make the light and made his way across the street and into the scaffolding entrance. Rest assured as he was, he looked down the shadowed sidewalk and saw the deli doors were open. He continued to make his way to the deli when he heard what he thought was an oversized truck roaring by as he got knocked to the ground.

Bright light streamed in as the covered scaffolding collapsed to the ground. Dust and debris scattered the area. Pete felt no sensation in his legs and was utterly immobilized. Muffled screams and yells echoed around him. Soon people came into his field of view and started to clear some of the rubble. Blood was splattered on bricks and the ground surrounding him. Looking up from the ground he saw a woman being carried away lifelessly that he recalled walking next to from the office.

Two men came over to him and started talking to him. He could not make out what they were saying in his delirious state but watched them. One of them held his head while the other started to clear some debris around his chest. The man clearing the debris turned and gave a dire sigh to the other man. The man holding Pete's head lowered it but doing so he tilted it up giving Pete an angle to see his lower abdomen. It had been completely severed in half by a massive section of rubble. Upon seeing this realization Pete gasped for breath and his eyes rolled back into his head. His world went black.

<<<<<<

...He continued the short walk and stood in horror across the street from where his favorite deli was supposed to be. The front of the tall building had the first several floors obscured with covered scaffolding. The building was evidently getting a makeover of some sort. Pete's heart sank and he wondered what he would do now for something to eat.

As he was looking up and down the street for other options, he noticed that the ends of the scaffolding were opened up and that foot traffic was still allowed in front of the building. As if by willing it into existence, someone exited the scaffolding exit across from him with an order from the deli in their hand indicating that the deli was indeed open.

Pulling out his phone to check the time he dropped some change. He felt he still had plenty of time and while he did not really need it, he picked up his change and waited for the next light. As he waited for the light, he was hit by a familiar wave of Déjà Vu. While he could not place it specifically, it gnawed at him as if it were of some importance.

Rubbing the back of his neck the walk sign lit up and started sounding off with the robotic voice of "Walk". Pete took one step off the curb when a loud crack caught his attention towards the scaffolding. Somewhere behind the curtains a large mass was falling. Pete along with many of the others on the street shouted for everyone to run, but it was no use. The mass came down way too quickly and with extreme force. Half of the scaffolding was torn down from eight floors up and the entire road was covered in debris.

Pete could not believe his eyes. He knew if he had made that first light that he would have been under all of that mess. He did not know when exactly, but sometime between telling people to get away and helping clear the debris the feeling of Déjà Vu finally subsided. He knew that he would not get the image of the man that was severed in half out of his head for some time...

Several weeks had gone by since Pete had his brush with death. He told his friend Jake about the whole incident, and they decided that to let off some steam they would go to the shooting range. Jake was a survivalist type. He collected a lot of different guns and liked to test them out at the range to see what functioned the best for himself, instead of taking a manufacturer's word, a magazine's guidance, or even online tutorial advice.

He liked to do hands-on self-testing. What Pete liked the most about it is that Jake provided all the ammo and range fees at no cost to himself. This always made it easy for Pete to agree to come. It was always a win-win deal.

The pair completed multiple sessions of firing at targets with pistols, rifles, and shotguns. Being an outdoor range there was plenty of space to set up the arsenal that Jake had brought. The metal targets provided instant feedback if you hit it with an audible 'ping'. Friendly competitions and bets were made throughout the morning as the two chose their firearms from the varied selection. The taunting back and forth between the two started to really cheer Pete up and he was beginning to forget all about the incident for once.

The two of them took a break for lunch and decided to clean the firearms as they were no longer going to use them after their break. Standing at the table Pete was cleaning a rifle and Jake was bringing over a couple pistols to start cleaning. Putting down one of the pistols, Jake started to disassemble the other and began to ask Pete how things were going with his girlfriend, Becca.

"You know she prefers Becky, jackass." Pete stated, correcting Jake.

"Yea, yea. I'll be sure to remember when I see her next. So? How're things?"

"They're good. We're going to her favorite place next week and then a movie later that night. She's been really supportive as well since the other week."

"That's great man. What movie ya seeing? Maybe I'll tag along. Oh, you don't need to clean these so we can eat off em. Just get the fresh carbon off."

"Ah. Well, I'm just taking care of it. And I'm not sure yet, I think she wants to see a new horror movie coming out. Having a problem with that?" Pete saw that Jake was having a little trouble with the second pistol while he began to reassemble the rifle.

"Nah, slides just a little tight. A little oil will help. That's awesome, maybe I will tag along. Glad she's not one of those chick-flick kinda girls. You buy the popcorn."

"Well, I'm not sure she'll want a third wheel, but you're we..."
BANG
The world suddenly vanished.

<<<<<<

The two of them took a break for lunch and decided to clean the firearms as they were no longer going to use them after their break. Standing at the table Pete was cleaning a rifle and Jake was bringing over a couple pistols to start cleaning. As Jake arrived and put down one of the pistols the eerie feeling of Déjà Vu once again began to swell within Pete. Jake started to disassemble the other pistol and began to ask Pete how things were going with his girlfriend, Becca.

"You know she prefers Becky, jackass." Pete said correcting Jake.

"Yea, yea. I'll be sure to remember when I see her next. So? How're things?

"They're good. We're going to her favorite place next week and then a movie later that night. She's been really supportive as well since the other week."

"That's great man. What movie ya seeing? Maybe I'll tag along. Oh, you don't need to clean these so we can eat off em. Just get the fresh carbon off."

"Ah. Well, I'm simply taking care of it. And I'm not sure yet, I think she wants to see a new horror movie coming out. Having a problem with that?" Pete noticed Jake having a little trouble with the second pistol while he began to reassemble the rifle.

"Nah, slides just a little tight. A little oil will help. That's awesome, maybe I will tag along. Glad she's not one of those chick-flick kinda girls. You buy the popcorn."

"Well, I'm not sure she'll...hey stop. That thing is pointed right at my head. Did you clear it?" The dreaded feeling of Déjà Vu reeled within him.

"Of course, I did. Look there's no magazine."

"That doesn't mean it's clear. You taught me that. Can you clear it properly?"

"I would if I could get the slide open. It's swelled shut or something. Here, let me take it to the firing line and prove it's empty."

Jake walked over to the firing line and aimed at a nearby target and pulled the trigger. *BANG* With a look of disbelief Jake lowered the pistol and turned to face Pete.

"Dude, I'm sorry." He fully cleared the pistol even after the slide locked back with a look of genuine concern. "I think I'm done for the day."

Pete felt the feeling of Déjà Vu cease, but he was convinced he was shot instead of how events actually transpired. He could not recall the specific sequence of events, but sensed something ominous was meant to occur if he did not speak up at the right moment. He could not help but ponder why these occurrences were becoming more frequent, and he sensed it was not the end of it.

>>>>>>

"We're already late. We gotta get moving Jake."

"We only got a few more blocks to go man. It's not my fault there's no parking near this place."

"Yea? Well, I told you that's why we should have gotten an Uber or something. Plus, I'm surprised she even agreed to let you come to dinner."

"I suppose it's my winning personality. Besides, I'm your wingman."

"I don't need a wingman. I'm not single and trying to pick up a girl."

"Then you're my wingman."

"We're going to dinner and a movie. You trying to pick up a waitress or an usher?"

"Yea, whatever. Hey, let's cut through here." Jake pointed down an alley. "This will cut the walk in half so we don't have to back track and I believe it pops out right next to the restaurant."

Pete looked down the alley and the wave of Déjà Vu hit him instantly. "Uh, no we can't."

"What do you mean we can't?"

"I mean we can't. Something down that way is bad news."

"Oh yea? And what kinda bad news are you talking about?"

"I don't know." Pete sighed. "I just know. Please listen and let's take the long way."

"You're talking crazy man. You already said we're late. Let's just go this way and get to eating."

"Dude, listen. You know these feelings of Déjà Vu I've been having, it's happening right now."

"IS THIS IN IT!!!" Jake yelled while throwing his hands up in the air wildly.

Pete groaned. "Strangely yes, but that is beside the point. When I've been having these feelings, I've had to forcibly choose another course of action or something bad happens."

"Like what?"

"Like the day on the street with the building collapsing, last week on the range when I knew there was a bullet in the chamber, and I think when I saw a deer on the way home a few weeks ago."

Jake's expression stopped looking amused after Pete discussed the range. "So, you're saying you knew something was wrong at the range?"

"Yes, and it's like I had already been through it. So, I knew what was going to happen, but not exactly what was going to happen."

Looking down the alley Jake began to reconsider his suggestion. He glanced at his watch. "Well, I guess we better pick up the pace lead foot. Can't keep your girl waiting all night."

The two continued down the sidewalk towards the intersection. The dark alley was illuminated by dim service lights. Dumpsters lined the edges of it down the entire length from the businesses whose names were scribbled on signs of the doors locked tight. Small alcoves for employees periodically placed throughout to get out the rain while they grabbed a smoke or took a break.

The alley was still and silent save the now hooded shadow slowly standing up from behind a dumpster only twenty feet from where Pete and Jake were talking on the sidewalk. Turning deeper into the alley a shimmer of light glinted off the blade in his hand from an alley light as he faded further into the darkness of the alley.

>>>>>>

Pete had a great night. Dinner with Becky and Jake was actually fantastic. The movie afterward was not disappointing and created some enjoyable conversation. To top it off Jake got the ushers number, which caught them all by surprise. It did help that she was also the bartender for this theater. Jake had even decided to stay until the bar closed to go someplace else with her to have drinks after she got off work. Pete and Becky decided to go back to his place.

They only had a foot in the door before Becky started to come on to Pete. It was like something out of a whole different kind of movie and Pete was enjoying it. They undressed all the way up the stairs, knocking over small tables and offsetting pictures on the wall. They giggled and continued kissing as they entered the bedroom commenced their love making. After a while, the two lay in each other's arms exhausted. Becky excused herself to the bathroom down the hall and suggested Pete get some drinks.

Taking a minute to compose himself he got up and walked down the hallway. At the top of the stairs, he knocked on the door to the bathroom asking Becky what she would like.

"WINE!" She giggled."

Turning to go downstairs Pete stepped on one of Becky's heeled shoes and twisted his ankle. He fell forward unable to catch himself on the wall or stair railing with the sudden momentum. He tumbled head over heels multiple times down the stairs. Landing with a loud crack and thud. He stared up into the darkness of his house dazed and confused lying naked on the floor in a contorted pose. The door at the top of the stairs flung open flooding the area in a pale-yellow glow. A scream filled the air as his vision faded.

<<<<<<

Taking a minute to compose himself he got up and walked down the hallway. At the top of the stairs, he knocked on the door to the bathroom asking Becky what she would like.

"WINE!" She giggled."

He was hit by the sensation of Déjà Vu yet again like a wave crashing onto the beach. He stopped dead in his tracks and slowly turned. Taking in his surroundings, he looked down and saw one of Becky's heeled shoes right at the top of the stairs. He bent down and picked it up and held it in his hands as he sat on his haunches.

The sound of a door opening broke his train of thought, and he slowly began to rise. Light flooding in blinded him in the darkness and he squinted his eyes to shield him from it. He heard feet scrambling from the bathroom.

WHITE! I WANT WHAAA..." Becky yelled not realizing that Pete was standing directly outside the door still as she slammed right into him. They both went tumbling down the stairs locked in an awkward embrace. Becky's screams silenced almost immediately on the first tumble onto the stairs as her neck broke.

Pete felt his shoulder shatter as he continued to fall head over heels down the stairs. He landed on his neck, the pain in his shoulder faded as he hit the landing. Becky's back was visible in front of him, indicating she lay across him, but he could not move his head under the weight of his and her bodies. His jaw was broken, preventing him from opening his mouth to yell for help; all he could manage was a groan. Trapped, he realized no one would be passing by for days.

Pete laid on the floor with his dead girlfriend draped across him for two more days unable to move, unable to get help. Only when his body was able to finally succumb to the trauma and dehydration was he able to welcome death. Pete believed he could almost see the hands of death reaching out to him as the darkness engulfed his sight.

<<<<<<

Taking a minute to compose himself he got up and walked down the hallway. At the top of the stairs, he knocked on the door to the bathroom asking Becky what she would like.

"WINE!" She giggled."

Pete froze as the feeling of Déjà Vu washed over him.

"No, this can't be."

Pete turned to run down the stairs. His eyes met an unfamiliar set looking into his own. Before him stood a man in a hooded jacket. He was unshaven with dark eyes and pale gaunt skin. In front of him he held a six-inch hunting blade.

"You knew I was there." The man whispered. "How did you know?"

"I don't what you're talking about." Pete muttered, raising his hands in the air. "Take whatever you want."

"I want to know how you KNEW!"

"I told you I don't..."

"WHITE! I WANT WHAAA..." The bathroom door flung open, and Becky came charging out. She bumped into Pete who fell into the man's knife that plunged into his upper abdomen. The blade cut deep into his heart, and he began to bleed out. The man was surprised not only by Becky coming out of the bathroom, but by the fact that his blade already had pierced his victim. Becky ran off to another room ran causing the man to panic. No longer wanting an answer from Pete he decided to run down the stairs and out of the house before the police could arrive.

Pete slumped against the railing as blood poured out of his abdomen. Putting his hand on the wound did nothing for the bleeding. While the feeling of Déjà Vu ended he realized that the man must have been in the alley that he and Jake were going to walk down for a short cut. As life began to fade from his eyes Becky opened the door to the bedroom with a bat in one hand and a phone in the other. Pete slumped over and fell down the stairs.

<<<<<<

"WINE!" She giggled."

Pete's head began to throb as he was hit with a case of Déjà Vu like a slap in the face.

"DAMN IT" he yelled. Becky called back in confusion as Pete ignored her as he paced back and forth on the upstairs landing. Thinking to himself why did it feel so strong? Why did his head hurt so badly? How many times had he been here? As he thought about it the images of him falling down the stairs became vivid images in his mind. He saw himself falling, he saw Becky falling, he saw a man creeping up behind him with a knife. an instance where he saw himself slicing his wrists at the front door. In another he killed the man, but dies of wounds, and many more. Screaming, he jumped the railing diving headfirst into his wood floor. His skull cracked and neck broke upon impact. The pain is excruciating yet brief as Pete's sight blinks out.

Pete groggily awoke. His eyes hurt and his vision was blurry. Unable to move his body or head, he discerned he was lying in a bed. He pondered which hospital he was in following his leap from the second story and how much time had elapsed since then. Above him, at the head of the bed, were machines unfamiliar to any hospital equipment he had encountered before.

The room was vast compared to a normal hospital room and looking up he saw large rotating fans and a white backlit tiled ceiling. Looking towards his feet, he observed multiple IV tubes leading into his body and back to unfamiliar machines. Beginning to panic slightly, he attempted to shift his head to glance around, only to realize it was strapped down to prevent movement. Nonetheless, he persisted in struggling.

After several attempts Pete was able to loosen the strap, but his head would still not move. He could not feel any pain, but it did feel like something was pressed up against his skull preventing him from turning in any direction. Pete gathered his strength and forced his head to turn to the left. Something snapped, and a sharp pain radiated on multiple spots on his head. Squeezing his eyes shut from the pain he only slightly perceived the sound of an odd alarm emitting from one of the machines.

Within a few moments the pain began to subside, and the sounds of bare feet started approaching Pete's bed.

"It would seem that someone has woken up." A very pleasant female voice sounded from behind Pete. It almost sounded like Becky.

Pete tried to speak and found that his throat did not have the ability to do so, and he could only groan. He must have severely damaged himself. First his vision, now his voice.

"You're quite calm, given your situation."

Pete found himself agreeing with the woman. Waking up in an unfamiliar hospital, vision degraded, unable to speak, unable to move, and prodded with all kinds of needles and hoses. The whole thing would be laughable if it were not serious. He wondered when he might leave. If he could manage to keep his eyes open long enough to look around without them hurting.

"Well, we will have to replace your stabilizer needles. You snapped those off. We will not be able to monitor you properly without those."

Pete started to feel a little better with the terminology being used. It made sense with the injuries he sustained. Now that the pain was starting to subside, he decided to try opening his eyes again. Opening his eyes, he saw another bed next to him. He started to focus on the person next to him, observing the same machines around them that were surrounding him.

As his eyes adjusted, he realized it was not one bed but rows of beds extending in multiple directions. His eyes widened. Despite the pain, Pete turned his head in the other direction and witnessed the same scene stretching out as far as he could see.

"Oh, there it is. I had not realized you had your eyes closed." The voice had moved to the head of his bed so he could not see her yet.

A four-fingered hand hovered over his head for a moment and the strap tightened more than it was previously causing Pete to groan in pain. He felt needles being removed from the sides of his head and new ones being inserted. While there was pressure there was no pain. He was unable to determine the depth the needles were being buried into his brain, nor could he figure out their size.

"Come now, you did this to yourself. Well, at least I believe you did. Let me check your chart."

A tall thin being with brownish-grey skin in a white translucent gown stood at Pete's shoulder, but he could not see its face. Pressing some symbols on the device, some melodic tones hummed and displayed some information in an unknown language. Pete once again tried to say something.

"You really need to stop trying to speak. You have never spoken before. Your body does not know how to make the words you are hearing. Your eyes hurt because you have never used them. Your kind always surprise me by breaking the needles and getting the strap loose. Your muscles are severely atrophied and underdeveloped, yet you still manage on occasion. You likely could not even walk out of here should you be able to get out of that bed. Let alone find an exit. Trust me, you're better off where you are."

"Ah, here it is. You got stuck on the Déjà Vu loop. This happens sometimes. When you unfortunately meet your end before your body here gives out the program simply resets a few minutes back and you take it the rest of the way. Most of the time it works out well, but sometimes...well this happens, and we have to do a reboot. Do not worry. You will only remember this as a figment of your imagination. You may even write about it as a work of fiction someday. Wouldn't that be great?"

Turning towards Pete the being resembled what many people refer to as the "Grey Men" aliens. It had big empty black eyes. A mouth that while it would open when it spoke it would not move normally. Its body was tall and slim and had elongated limbs and appeared to be able to work its equipment telekinetically as well as physically.

"Well now, you are all set to return. Your protocols have been adjusted. Please do be mindful of your decisions. Not that you will remember. Reboot: Indigo Nero Four Six Nine Four Seven Limbo Plato"

Pete's head began to split as his vision was blinded with an unbearable light. Though his eyes were shut it pierced though his eyelids. The pain in his head radiated worse than any migraine he had ever experienced. The white now swirled with colors. Flashes of images came to him in rapid succession. Images of what he had just been through or had he? As quickly as they appeared they were gone. The images that appeared were burning away in the searing white light. His head throbbed as the images burned away. More images appeared and disappeared. As the images were almost becoming overwhelming the light winked out.

<<<<<<

Leaving the office after another average day of work meant Pete would take his normal route down the back roads to avoid all the evening traffic. While it may take ten or fifteen extra minutes, he enjoyed the scenery it provided. It was fall and the leaves were starting to change so the drive was more enjoyable this time of the year.

3:4:9-VIII:X:XII:XIII-F:G:I:J:K

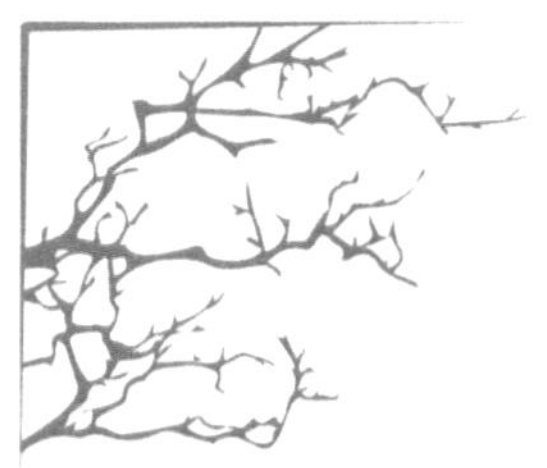

Oppression

The sun had only been in the sky for a couple of hours and yet the heat of the day was already sweltering. Tensions were running high with all the new restrictions being emplaced by the ruling dictator and no one dared to speak out against him despite everyone knowing it was wrong. No one was willing to risk their lives with the police and the dictator's own personal army taking care of any outspoken opposition. No one, until today.

Fatima had had enough and many of her friends in college also felt the same way. They had decided that today was going to be the day they would demand free and fair elections and for the dictator to accept the outcome and free political rivals from prison. Her small group of nearly thirty students filled the courtyard of the local government building they chose to protest. While they wanted to do it at the palace, this location gave them more time for exposure before the police arrived.

Many students filmed the demonstration, and those who were able, live-streamed the event so that as many people as possible could watch. They all knew that the people had had enough, and someone was willing to stand up against the regime. Fatima was risking more than just being arrested due to the lack of rights women had. However, she knew she had to be at the front of the demonstration so that women's voices were also to be heard.

The protest had been carrying on for almost an hour when the police began to arrive. The officers kept their distance at first, only shouting for the students to cease and desist and leave the area. Fatima and her friends only continued more fervently in defiance. She started to feel a little fear creeping up inside her, but the determination of what they came to do outweighed that fear. They would continue until they could no longer maintain their dominance.

After a brief time of the police not advancing the students became more emboldened in their political stance and tried to rally passing spectators. The police line parted as reinforcements arrived dressed in riot gear. Again, they demanded the students to disperse and leave the area.

The students stood in solidarity as the police began to march forward with batons and shields in hand. Tear gas began to be thrown into their group causing many of the students to cough, tear up, and become disoriented. The large group began to disband into smaller cells trying to maintain their protest as long as possible.

Fatima found herself with a group of five students along the outside of the courtyard wall. A couple of the students were still filming despite their issues with the tear gas. Along the street in front of them people ran to avoid the gas and police. She realized they were quickly losing their advantage. As she turned to discuss what they should do when they all heard shots ring out from the direction of the police. Fatima felt a slap to her head as they all grabbed one another and dropped to the ground taking cover.

Standing back up she had a ringing in her ears. She tried to clear the fogginess from the slap, dropping down, and getting up in such haste. Shaking off the haze she saw some her group start running off. Looking back the police started walking out of the gas and smoke. Gasping, she turned to run and the sight at her feet caught her eye.

A student from her group was kneeling down on the ground ignoring the police. He was holding Fatima's lifeless body in one arm while filming with the other. He cried while trying to get out the message that she had be killed. He looked up and realized the police were getting close and apologized to Fatima's lifeless body as he put her down and ran away.

Kneeling down at her body she felt a great sadness wash over her. A sadness that she will not be able to make a difference any longer. A sadness of failure. Looking deep into her own dead eyes she saw a reflection of the riot police simply walking around her body. No emotion pouring out of their mask covered faces about what had happened to her. Shields lifted and batons readied, they marched past her without so much a passing glance as they continued to clear out the remaining students.

As she looked away from her body the street and courtyard began to shift into a lavish garden. Looking around even the police began to vanish into various shrubs and rows of trees as the street below their feet turned to grass and sprang new life. Glancing back down her body had been replaced by a moss-covered log ripe with mushrooms. Realizing there was no longer ringing in her ears she heard footsteps approaching from behind.

A man as gorgeous as can be stood before her. His bronze skin reflected the surrounding light as he walked toward her. He had black flowing hair and a well-trimmed beard. He was dressed in traditional white robes and wore brown leather sandals. Had his eyes not been entirely black Fatima would have never guessed the man to be an angel.

"Who..." she asked.

"*I am Azrael. I am here to escort you to Barzakh.*" His voice was calm and serene regardless of his tongue of fire and the harmonious tones that echoed at every word.

"What happens after that?" she questioned half worried and half intrigued.

"*What happens is different for all. You all meet the creator for judgement and your outcome will determine your status here within Barzakh. You are already here within the gardens, so you should have a pleasant stay as we wait.*"

"What are we waiting for?"

"*For Israfel to blow his trumpet. Barzakh is not your final resting place. Nor is it your final judgement. Only after the trumpet sounds and all life ends and begins anew will everyone find their rightful place.*"

"What if I weren't in the gardens right now?"

"*You would be boiling in the cauldrons, drowning in the rivers of blood, or even shackled and experiencing unspeakable tortures until that time.*"

"Then I am forever grateful."

"*As you should be. Here you will meet with your relatives and live the life that could be.*"

"You mean I might end up elsewhere?"

"*Of course, you will be questioned at dawn and dusk each day. Your faith will be tested daily. Should you falter, your status may change and after the trumpets it will be up to the prophets to beg Allah on your behalf for Intersession into paradise.*"

"I will not falter. My faith will always stand."

"*All confess as much. Many fail.*"

Azrael turned and motioned for Fatima to follow through the gardens. As they walked people began to appear that she recognized from her life and from before her life that she had only seen in pictures. While she waved, they only looked at her for a moment as she walked by. The expression they gave was indifferent but suggested they would not engage her until her judgement was determined.

The gardens became more lavish as they walked. Fruit of all varieties blossomed from the trees, the cups people drank from never seemed to empty, and the food that was sitting out did not seem to spoil. Joyous conversation and laughter filled the air along a symphony of fragrances that danced and intermingled, it created a sensory masterpiece for those fortunate to wander its lush pathways.

The gardens were lit with a beautiful light that came from everywhere even though it was dense and should not have allowed so much to come through. Looking through the canopy the sun was not visible to Fatima, but the light radiated at every turn. No step was faltered though the ground was uneven in many places and after walking for an exceptionally long time she had not grown tired or weary in the slightest.

If this was only a glimpse into what paradise was supposed to be Fatima was determined to keep her faith strong. To keep the faith of her family strong. She wanted to make sure they would be able to be there with her when that time came. Though she had felt saddened by her death and her earthly purpose failed, that life had passed, and she had a new purpose, and she would be successful.

Azrael came to a stop standing before an entrance to a large grove. It was gated with wooden doors entwined with vines and light weaving intricate patterns within the wood. He waved, motioning for her to come forward with an open welcoming hand.

"I can go no further. The path ahead is now yours alone. Should your judgement reflect a decision contrary to your current state, I will be here waiting to escort you further into Barzakh. Go forth."

Fatima took a deep breath and gathered herself, her heart pounding with anticipation as she stood before the threshold. She knew she was about to meet the creator, and every fiber of her being urged her to stay resolute, to show her worth as a faithful servant. With a silent prayer of gratitude to Azrael, she reached for the golden handle on the door, her hand trembling slightly with nerves. As she pushed it open, a radiant light engulfed her, suffusing the grove with an ethereal glow that wrapped around her like a comforting embrace. Stepping forward, she left the familiar tranquility of the gardens behind, her resolve unwavering as she prepared to face the divine judgement that awaited her beyond the threshold.

1:4:5:6:8:12-IX-A:C:D:E:F:G:H:K

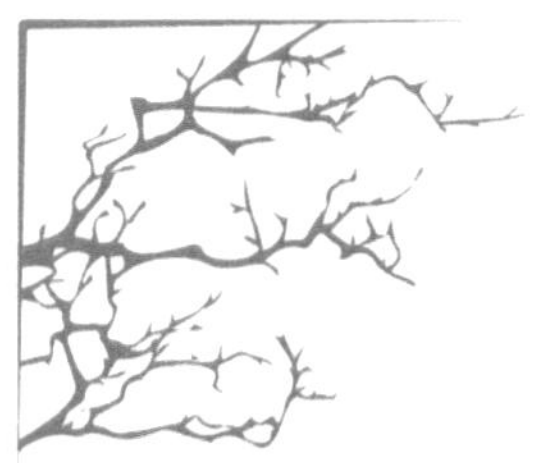

A Good Boy

The ball flew through the air landing in the grass at the far side of the yard. Spunky rushed to snatch it up like he did many times before. He could do this all day long if his people would let him. Repeatedly, he chased the ball and brought it back to his big man. The big man was starting to look tired even though they had only been playing for five minutes.

This was his favorite part of the day and looked forward to it every day when the big man got home from wherever he went while he napped. The man stopped throwing the ball to bend over and scratch Spunky's head a moment. Though he did not want to stop chasing the ball the opportunity for scritches was something he would not pass up.

His ears perked up as the sound of the big grey bus bringing home his boy and girl. Spunky barked happily as he ran around the side of the house to meet them at the fence. He jumped gleefully as they came through to greet him. Giggling and laughing they pet him and scratched his belly as he rolled over onto his back. Rolling over he chased after his boy and girl through the yard. He loved to play with them and could do it all day long. This was certainly his favorite part of the day.

"Good boy, Spunky." They all said. "Let's go in."

Spunky replied with a bark after playing for five minutes and followed them into the house. Inside he lifted his nose in the air and sniffed. His big lady was beginning to cook the food for their meal. It sure smelled great. The smells and food the came from the eating room were amazing. He hoped that his boy would not forget to drop a piece or two later.

He followed his big man to the sitting room and laid next to his chair. The man reached down and gave him a few scritches before he fell asleep. Spunky decided he would also take a nap since no one wanted to play right now.

Spunky woke up as food was being served. He trotted over to his bowls and found they had already been filled and started to devour it immediately. He loved the soft food his people gave him. It always tasted better than the hard food even though it was not too bad either. After he finished, he sat at the table next to his boy and waited.

Almost immediately after sitting down something fell from the table. Spunky ate it so fast he barely chewed it, but knew it was a delicious piece of meat. He anxiously waited for another piece. As usual another item fell from the table. Spunky quickly started to chew it up. However, this time he stopped before he swallowed and spit out whatever it was. Looking down at it the thing looked like a tiny tree. Looking up at his boy he wondered why he would give him this grey piece of nastiness. It must have been a mistake. Despite the mistake, Spunky walked away from the table back to the sitting room to lay down and take an after-meal nap.

Five minutes later Spunky was awakened by the big man to go for a walk. He bounced with excitement as this was his favorite thing to do. He got to say hello to his friends, and watch the nightly people parade, and if he was lucky chase a dumb cat or maybe even a bunny. This night, however, there were no cats or bunnies to be seen. He was not happy about that.

Spunky did have some satisfaction though, as he always did when he defecated. He stared up at his big man who would always tell him to stop for some reason. Spunky was not sure why, he just wanted to make sure the big man was looking out for him when he was vulnerable. He also found it very awkward that the big man picked up his poop after he was finished. His people were weird, but he was always told he was a "Good Boy" after he finished. That always made him feel good.

Getting back to the house the lights were out and his boy and girl had gone to sleep. The big man took off his leash and hung it on a hook and began to go upstairs to his sleeping room. Spunky followed up after and jumped up on the bed and laid down to go to sleep as well. He watched the big man and lady get ready to go to sleep.

The big lady put on her favorite grey skin blanket that was really big and the big man only had on some leg covers that showed most of his human undercoat. It was odd to Spunky that the man always covered it up in the day with a various skin blankets. They looked funny to Spunky, but he loved them all the same. After playing with sticks in their mouths and spitting water out they got into the bed and turned off the lights. Spunky closed his eyes and fell asleep.

It had only been about five minutes when Spunky woke up to a strange smell. He stretched and hopped down from the bed. His paws hit the soft floor lightly with an intent to not wake his people. He followed the scent down the stairs and started noticing black clouds along the upside-down ground part of the room. Turning into the eating room he saw flames billowing up from where the big lady makes the food. The fire was starting to engulf the wooden boxes around it. Spunky got close to it and barked at it. It was hot and he knew it was bad. He knew he had to get the big man.

Spunky sprinted up the stairs barking. Running into the sleeping room he leaped on the bed and onto the big man. Barking at the big man he awoke immediately confused and looked a little upset. The big lady also woke up though Spunky did not mean to wake her up.

"What do you want boy?" As the big man asked Spunky as a loud ringing noise started to go off all over the house. It drove Spunky crazy and he couldn't think straight.

"Honey, I smell smoke." the big lady said.

"Go get the kids. C'mon boy."

Spunky followed the big man as the big lady went down the hallway. The big man coughed as they went down the stairs. The clouds were much thicker than before. Turning the corner to the eating room the big man stopped. He grabbed Spunky by his neck-ring and stopped him from running into the flames that had now spread to the entire eating room.

"Good boy, Spunky. Honey! We got to go!"

The big lady came down the stairs with his boy following behind. The big man turned, and they all ran for the door to the outside. Spunky could not see his girl. He began to get scared and did not run for the door.

"C'mon boy." The big man urged from the open door.

Spunky stamped his front paws, turned, and ran back up the stairs. He heard the big man yell for him from downstairs, but he needed to find his girl. Running into her sleeping room he saw that she was not in her bed or under it. He ran to check the boys' room and could not find her there. He thought to himself, *why would the big lady forget his girl.*

He checked the big people's room and still there was no girl and decided to try downstairs again. Running to the stairs he was prepared to jump down as a loud crash caused him to cower back as the upside-down ground collapsed is a crash of fiery wood blocking them.

Spunky ran back over to his girls' room and checked again for her. He whimpered when he could not find her. Remembering that he sometimes looked out the window when the grey bus brought her home, he jumped up to view outside. Spunky saw his people in the street, and there was his girl.

Spunky was relieved to see her and barked happily to see she was all right. His people looked up and appeared to be yelling at him. His boy and girl were crying. Tilting his head, he was not sure why they were sad. He was a good boy and got them out from the fire. The big man told him.

Spunky continued barking at the window for five minutes when he started to feel tired. He began to hack from the smoke and began feeling very weak. Crawling under his girls' bed and into the corner he curled into a ball. Black clouds filled her room, and he was no longer able to see out the window. Feeling very weak and unable to open his eyes any longer, Spunky thought to himself, "I'm a good boy," as his breath ceased.

The last few weeks went by in a blur for the small pup. He did not have a name and loved being with his siblings. He wondered why they were all now in a box and away from their mother. Regardless, they played in the box. One by one his brothers and sisters disappeared while he played and took five-minute naps. As he awoke from his latest nap, he found he was the last one in the box. Two figures stood over the box and reached in to scratch his head and rub his belly.

"He's so cute dad."

"Can we get him?"

"I don't know, kids."

"Honey, it's been almost a year now."

"Yea, dad. We miss Spunky."

The little pup barked with enthusiasm as he suddenly remembered that name. As the people moved around the box, he also began to recognize his boy and his girl. He bounced around the box joyfully. He barked and played with the two kids as the man talked. He remembered that this was his favorite part of the day.

"Well, I suppose. What are we gonna name him?"

"Spunky Two!" The kids responded in unison.

"I think Spunky will work just fine."

With a wag of his tail, Spunky looked back one last time at the box he had called home, his heart momentarily ached at the loss of his brothers and sisters. As the big man gently lifted him out, Spunky's eyes sparkled with anticipation, eager to embark on this new chapter of his life filled with endless adventures and boundless joy. Together, they walked away, watching the people parade around them.

2:3:6-II:VI:XIII

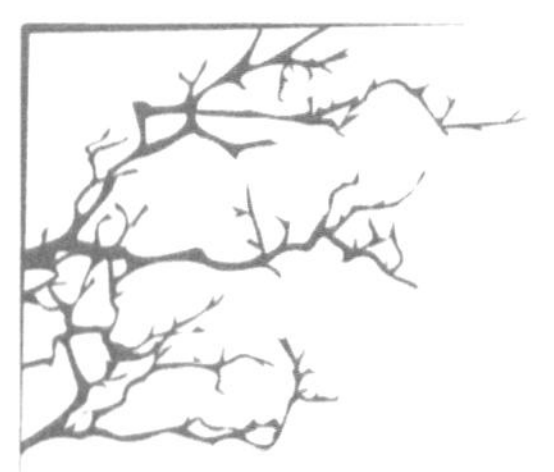

Death Row

They said Pierre Faucher was crazy. That his science would achieve nothing. However, unlike all the other vivisectionists in his field, he was willing to demonstrate the effectiveness of his work. Simply getting the occasional reactionary response from a rabbit or rat test subject by prodding dying organs or a final reaction from criminals, who were not likely to participate in science after being beheaded anyhow, did not guarantee results. Also, having the condemned agree before being executed did not quantify the data. The last thoughts going through a criminal's mind would be that of redemption, regret, anger, family, or that of many different things. Most of which would not be to support the betterment of science.

Pierre had to do something else to prove his theories. He had to take matters into his own hands. All vivisectionists have been able to prove so far that organs function for a time after being removed from the body. Limbs and the brain seem to function as well, to a degree, after being separated from the body if even for a short time.

Pierre wanted to prove that despite being decapitated the brain still functioned enough to comprehend their environment and respond in simple ways like blinking, smiling, looking in specific directions, and opening and closing one's mouth. Speaking, unfortunately, was not possible due to separation of the vocal cords and lungs providing a means of pushing air through the mouth and throat.

Yes, now was his time to prove to his colleagues just how brilliant he was. A crowd was gathering to observe the spectacle and began to cheer as the executioner came into sight at the back making his way to the platform. Looking into the crowd Pierre could see some of his fellow vivisectionists also there to witness the experiment. Pierre called his assistant who was preparing the basket by the guillotine along with the small writing table with some blank pages of parchment for taking notes for the experiment. His apprentice looked very anxious about his role to lose his head. Even though Pierre had offered to financially care for the family of anyone who volunteered he knew it would be difficult for anyone to take on this experiment.

"Is everything ready?"

"Yes, Dr. Faucher. Is there anything else I can assist with before the experiment begins?"

"No, no. Go ahead and stand by the guillotine. The executioner is here, and it is time for my speech." The apprentice moved towards the guillotine as the cheering in the crowd grew livelier as the executioner reached the platform. Pierre greeted him and using his arms motioned for the people to quiet down for him to speak.

"Ladies and gentlemen, I thank you for your audience this evening. You are all about to be a part of something revolutionary in the pursuit of science..."

"William Barthalamew Duncan, also known as 'The Dreaded Duncan.' For the crimes you have committed in the name of the King under God, you are to be hanged by the neck until dead. You are guilty of piracy, murder, smuggling, lewd acts of indecency in public, blaspheming the Kings name, attempted robbery of the royal treasury, horse theft..."

The list continued as Duncan looked among the crowd in front of him as he smiled a toothless grin. The list of crimes against him seemed to be mostly true even if some of the charges were slightly embellished. He closed his one good eye thinking back on some of the crimes as they were listed.

He did his best to stifle his laughter due to his hands being bound behind him and his neck fixed with a rope securely around it. Closing his eyes did little to block out the light of the sun beaming down on him. He wished they would do this at night rather than midday, so that he would at least go out with some comfort.

Hearing a specific crime, he had been waiting for, Duncan spoke up, "Ye should have been there for that one, lieutenant. Then at least ye be hanging me as a friend and not a stranger." Duncan stated as he raised his foot to scratch his calf. "I believe you were stationed there at that point, Ah, that's right. You were passed out drunk with me girl Matilda. She do be a wily one. In fact, one time, she..."

"Stand still and keep your mouth shut unless asked to speak. Don't force me pull the lever early." The executioner warned as he kicked the back of Duncan's knees causing them to buckle briefly. The rope tightened around his neck causing him to choke momentarily until he regained his footing. "Much better."

"...as declared by his royal highness the King. Do you have anything to say for yourself Mr. Duncan?"

"Well..." Duncan paused as he looked back at the executioner briefly before continuing. "First, that be Captain Duncan. I may be your prisoner, but I still have me title even if I no longer be on me ship." Duncan stared at the lieutenant dropping all air of tomfoolery he had recently been presenting. "And the second thing, I plead guilty to all these charges you hang over me head and around me neck."

"Well, that is a little surprising. So be it, Captain." The lieutenant rolled up his papers and signaled for Father Mathias to come forward and offer a final prayer for the prisoner.

Buford stood in the blistering sun with the blindfold covering his sight. Sweat had already soaked through the thin fabric and stung his eyes each time he tried to open them. He had been walking for hours since the sun came up. Had he and the two other men he was chained to not been blindfolded they could probably get to the garrison faster. Buford assumed at least one of them was a Johnny Reb. Ahead Buford heard a bugle call for evening mess.

"Looks like we made it in time for dinner Captain."

"We don't eat until we process the prisoners first." Captain Miller ordered. "Leave them outside the gates until I process the paperwork with the commander. I'll ride inside to expedite the process. Sergeant, see it done." He rode off from the rest of the group.

"Yes sir. Line 'em up private. Prisoners, remove your blindfolds no need for you to have em on any longer. Won't be able to find your way out of here without running into one of our outposts anyhow. So don't even think about it." His thick Scottish accent was hard to understand most of the time, but Buford was certain he understood most of what was being said, so he removed his blindfold.

Looking around Buford found the familiar garrison wall still marred with arrows and charred with ash from recent attacks. The terrain surrounding the garrison was flat and open for several hundred yards before any tree line. It was favorable should they decide to run, but also favorable for any sharpshooters to pick them off. Looking down at the irons around his ankle there were a total of five of them on the link. Even if they worked together, it would be disastrous to travel anywhere with this many. Let alone the six Union soldiers that surrounded them and their blistered bare feet.

"Get in line." The sergeant shouted. The five men shuffled as best they could to straighten the line they were already in to avoid a beating. The soldiers tied off their horses at the water trough beside the gate and began filling tin cups. "Hurry up with those drinks." The soldiers moved down the line passing out the cups to the prisoners. No one dared raising a cup until ordered to do so despite the thirst that welled within them.

Burford waited patiently for the order and drank the contents completely once it was given. As he drank, he noticed a single rider in the distance looking in their direction. He struggled to determine any detail except for his long coat remaining still while the wind kicked up dust around him. Something felt off about the rider, but he was unaware what it was. From this distance, he spotted a rifle jutting out of the saddle, indicating he was likely one of the sharpshooters conducting a perimeter check.

The gates swung open as the captain walked through with another officer. Buford recognized the adjutant as Major Banks. He was the Colonels right hand man and, in his absence, made the decisions needed to keep the garrison running. He carried a list with him as he approached the chained men.

"Captain, as the Colonel stated, we only have space for two prisoners due to the recent attacks. List your prisoners and their offense and I'll decide which we will harbor. Begin."

"Prisoner one: Lyle Black, farmer: housing and feeding rebel soldiers. Prisoner two: Buck Boyle, rebel private. Prisoner three: Buford Stamp, deserter. Prisoner four, name withheld, suspected rebel soldier residing at the Black farm. Prisoner five: Moon Shadow, Blackfoot Indian warrior."

"I'm no Blackfoot" Moon Shadow growled.

"Silence!" The sergeant struck the man in the gut causing him to double over then pulled him by the hair to stand him back up. "Or I'll scalp you where you stand."

"That's enough Sergeant." The captain stated. "This is our list, Major. Take the time you need to make a decision Sir."

"No need Captain, I've already decided. Prisoners four and five will be questioned. The other three will face a firing squad at dawn."

"As ordered sir. Sergeant, see that the two prisoners are sent to the brig. The other three will remain out here for the evening with a rotating guard."

"Aye sir."

Buford was not fazed by the order. He knew what was in store for him. The Private next to him was maybe sixteen years old and began to cry. He had no words for him as he fought for the side that still enslaved his family. The farmer was in shock and could not believe he was being put to death. He pled for his life as the two officers went back into the garrison. His pleas were ignored as he crumbled to the ground next to the private.

Dusk was settling in as the soldiers staked the prisoners to the ground and set in the perimeter. Another set of soldiers came through the gate and brought the others as well as the prisoners their dinner. Outside the perimeter Buford watched the dark rider pass by closer, his face shrouded by his hood. He could not tell who it was by the horse but was sure at this distance that there was something familiar about the man. As the man rounded the corner of the garrison one of the soldiers shouted to Buford to finish his meal or he would sleep on an empty stomach. Trying to push the thought of his impending doom out of his mind Buford finished his meal and laid down to sleep. Pulling his cap down over his eyes he let the rhythmic sobbing of the boy and farmer lull him to sleep.

Luis ate his steak medium with no sauce and some seasoned fries. He was allowed a non-alcoholic beer to accompany his meal, but decided water was all he would drink. The television played a movie that Luis could enjoy with his meal had he wanted to enjoy it. Instead, Luis had the TV muted and ate his meal in silence and contemplated what he would say in the upcoming moments. Despite his steak being juicy it lacked any taste on his tongue as he chewed in silence.

Several knocks came at the heavy door to the small cream-colored room. As the locking mechanism unlatched a familiar face stepped through the door. "It's time Luis. You ready?" Once through the door it closed with a metallic clank and a muted buzzer sound from the opposite side.

"I don't think anyone can truly be ready for this Clay, but I'm about as ready as I can be." Luis stood up from the table and moved over to the door. Stopping in front of Clay, he lifted his hands in front of himself holding them at his waist.

"Unfortunately, this is required. I know you won't run, but we still have to put 'em on."

"It's fine Clay."

"For what it's worth, I believe you Luis. All this time in here and never causing an issue, knowing what was coming. I'd say that proves your innocence." Clay proceeded to put Luis in his prison restraints.

"Thanks. However, I never caused any issue, because I deserved this punishment, not because of my innocence." Luis waited for the restraints to be secured before lowering his hands. Clay moved to stand behind Luis and pulled out his nightstick to bang twice on the door.

The door buzzed and clicked once again opening to reveal Warden James and Father David in the hallway.

"Time to go Luis. This way please." The warden gestured down the hall.

"Yes sir. Father, may I have my last rites as we walk?" Luis asked as he began moving in the direction the warden indicated.

"Of course, Luis." Father David began to recite the last rites as the four of them walked in a somber procession down the hall. Save for the rattling of his chains, the footfalls made Luis think as if he were marching to his end instead of being led to his demise.

Reaching another large heavy door Clay reached forward to bang on it with his nightstick. "Luis, do you accept the Lord, Jesus Christ into your heart and ask for his forgiveness?"

"As I have every day, but also for my brother, Father."

"I cannot promise anything for your brother as he is no longer here, but I will pray for you both." Father David concluded the last rites as the door unlocked and opened allowing them all to move inside the cold, unforgiving chamber The tight quarters and muted grey walls enhanced the sense of confinement within the room. Luis immediately felt the weight of his decision coming down on him.

"Luis, are you sure you want to do it this way?" The warden asked. "I can call the governor and request a stay of execution for lethal injection instead."

"No need Warden James. This is my punishment, and this is how I choose to fulfill it."

"Alright Luis. It is your decision." The warden motioned for Clay and the other guard that was in the room already to begin strapping Luis into the chair. "Do not mess this up gentleman. We are one of the last facilities that still has one of these and despite the end result we can still get fried for screwing it up in the end." The warden winced, realizing what he had said. "Luis, I'm sorry, that was..."

Luis grinned regardless of the grim situation. "It was poor timing, but no need to apologize."

The warden moved over to the phone and checked the connection and volume of the ringer. "I don't foresee the Governor calling, but just in case."

Clay and the other guard finished prepping Luis in the chair and nodded toward the warden.

"Alright Luis, time for the feral dogs." The warden signaled Clay, who hit a switch that moved a curtain obstructing the view to the room on the other side of the glass. The room where the family of all the victims were currently residing, whose eyes all now turned to Luis.

"...And that dear friends is why being here to witness this event is more than simply witnessing an execution. It is for the pursuit of science. It is for the..." Pierre's assistant's repeated coughing finally drew his attention. His assistant looked at him with pleading eyes and raised eyebrows. He darted his eyes towards the spectators then back to Pierre. The doctor looked out at the audience and this time he truly looked. When had he started his speech, was it five, ten minutes ago? Thirty? How long had it been since dusk had past when the executioner had arrived? Looking over at his fellow scientists it appeared that even they were growing impatient.

"But enough of all that. You came for a demonstration and a demonstration I will give. Francois, please take your position in the device." Cheering erupted among the crowd as the assistant positioned himself behind the guillotine and was strapped in by the executioner.

"Dr. Faucher, my note is in your journal. There is also a letter for my family." Francois said solemnly trying to look up at Pierre.

"Yes, thank you my boy. They will get it." Pierre picked up his journal and pulled out the folded piece of parchment. Raising his voice once again, "My assistant has written specific instructions on what to tell him once post-cranial severance has occurred. At which time the subject experiences a cessation of cerebral and physiological functions which demarcates a point of irreversible separation between the cephalic and corporeal components, engendering an unequivocal state of biological cessation." Expecting cheers and awes Pierre once again looked at the crowd who were baffled at his explanation.

"Ahem, As I was saying, once his head has been removed from his body I will read the instructions and like you I do not know what he has written until I read it aloud after." The crowd roared as he took a position on the opposite side of the guillotine from the executioner and signaled that they were ready. "Remember to be quick with retrieving the specimen please."

"Yes doctor, I will pick up the head right after."

"Ugh...specimen." Pierre grumbled.

The executioner teased the crowd with false pulls of the lever. He then got them riled up with a final triumphant pull that caused the razor-sharp blade to plummet the short distance to sever the assistant's head from his body and land in the provided basket. The executioner picked up the head and pointed it towards the doctor as the crowd cheered.

"Not towards me you buffoon. Towards the other scientists. I'll be able to see from where I stand." The executioner pivoted slightly and pointed the face of the apprentice out towards the spectators. Silence fell over them as they gazed upon the head instead of it simply being in the basket.

"Francois, look at me!" Pierre commanded as the lifeless eyes of the head slowly lulled forward looking at Pierre. A gasp came from the spectators that could see and a woman fainted in the front row. The other scientists looked unimpressed.

Unfolding the piece of paper quickly Pierre read aloud. "Wink and smile!" Pierre looked intently at Francois' face for sign of movement. "WINK AND SMILE!" He shouted again. Still there was no movement. The eyes began to shift downward as they started to close. "NO! FRANCOIS! LOOK AT ME!" Pierre shook the executioner's hands holding the head. "LOOK AT ME!" He slapped his apprentice's face, but no movement occurred save his mouth being jarred open by the force.

"Such a waste of time." One scientist said.

"I thought there was to be a breakthrough." Another protested.

"Such a disappointment." A third chimed in as they began to turn and walk away.

Pierre was devastated. Looking out at the spectators he saw that they too were more disturbed by the demonstration than appeased by it. This was supposed to be his moment. Why had it not worked? His apprentice was completely sold on the idea. His family was to be taken care of, and...wait. Pierre realized that his apprentice must have had his family on his mind in the end more than the experiment and thus caused the issue. However, how was that going to fix anything? Then it came to him.

"STOP! You didn't think that was the end of the demonstration did you? Doctors, if you would join me up here for the FINAL demonstration."

"Where is the test subject? Dr. Faucher? I do not see any other apprentices." The other scientists laughed.

"Why, you are looking at him." The scientists gasped, as the crowd that had stopped to listen began to cheer. Pierre bent over to grab his pen and scratched out his apprentice's note and made one of his own on the piece of parchment. "Now, do not read this until after the event. We do not want to spoil the surprise."

Pierre made his way to the backside of the guillotine. The executioner had already moved Francois' body despite his own surprise. Pierre got into the guillotine and looked over to the executioner. "I think we have held everyone up long enough. Have them give a countdown from three and pull."

"If that is what you desire doctor." The executioner quickly explained to the crowd faster than Pierre thought he would. It must have been a more customary practice than he was familiar. The executioner moved back to the guillotine and began the count.

"Three" The crowd roared with anticipation.

"Two" Pierre reflected on the note he had written.

"One" The executioner placed his hand on the lever.

Captain Duncan stood defiantly as Father Mathias started his prayer. With all the cruelty that he was able to get away with and the other atrocities he saw among his voyages on the sea, Duncan could not bring himself to believe in such a just God. The priest continued to pray regardless of all the evil that ran rampant. He himself ran unchecked for years causing a great amount of misery for many settlements as his men left few alive to tell the tale of their savagery.

His men were unaware that Duncan had been planning most of his plundering for years as a captive. The very people they pillaged, he waged his own personal war against, but it was no excuse for the brutality that he brought upon the innocents there. However, he was blinded by the rage of the captivity, the murder of his family, and the killing of his former crew. Everyone that left him for dead. For the Dreaded Duncan no one was to be forgiven and upon his escape he made sure they all would fear the seas as long as he roamed free.

Father Mathias finished his prayer. As he left the platform he paused briefly in front of Captain Duncan to offer a final prayer of contrition below him and left the courtyard as the death drums began to beat. The hangman circled the platform to take his position near the release lever. "When the final toll of the bell rings out, so shall the release of the lever." The lieutenant ordered as the hangman nodded in acknowledgement. Bass drums beat out a steady rhythm awaiting the toll of the bell.

Thump...thump, thump. Thump...thump, thump. It beat for several minutes leading up to noon day toll. For Duncan it was an eternity. Watching out above the port he watched the sea come into the harbor and disappear into the horizon the bell begun its noon day chime. He watched as a large merchant ship was leaving the harbor with others prepping at the docks. He longed to be on one of those ships again, but he knew within the minute he would be hanging and gasping for his final breaths.

The drums began a rapid beat as the chimes began to ring throughout the courtyard. Duncan watched as the crowd edged closer to one another in anticipation. The lieutenant watched on uninterested looking more at the scenery than at Duncan. He could have spit had his mouth have not gone dry at being ignored by such a petty officer. Stifling his anger, he watched as the back of the crowd was beginning to split from the back to the front. Someone was coming. As the final chime rang both Duncan and the hangman saw who it was and saw he had his hand up in a pausing gesture.

"Why have you not pulled the lever hangman? What are you doing? What is going..." The lieutenant cut himself short as he saw Admiral Baylor standing before the platform. "Sir, my apologies I did not think you would be..." The lieutenant was cut off by the admiral's sudden gaze.

"Perhaps, if you would take your duties more seriously you would have noticed my arrival as I entered the courtyard. You are dismissed lieutenant."

"Uh...yes sir." The young officer left the platform with haste as the admiral climbed the stairs stopping in front of Duncan.

"It has been a long time Captain Duncan is it?" The admiral asked keeping his voice in a whispered tone.

"Not long enough."

"True, and to think I almost missed this had I not recognized you as you came through processing. The beard, and lack of teeth make you look older, and the eye patch almost unfamiliar, but your voice is what gave you away. I genuinely thought you were dead all these years."

"It wasn't like I weren't trying, but I had unfinished business." Duncan's whispered voice lost all account of the seafaring accent that he had previously been speaking with towards the crowd. "Besides, you're the one to thank for my new looks."

"Yes, I suppose I am. However, you ruined a lot of opportunities for me. No matter, they were only delayed and now that you will be dead I will be back in business."

"I wouldn't count on that old man."

"Oh? And why is that?

"You didn't kill all my loyal crew. My first mate lives. His word and documents of what you've done are on their way to the King as we speak."

"Is that so?" The admiral smiled. "And how would that be? How could you know that when you have been in custody here for weeks and have never had access to any of my documents since you went rogue?"

"Why, he was here today and has been even longer than I have. You see when people think you're dead no one cares to recognize you unless you make it known for the most part. You see, he gave me my last rites."

"Father Mathias? No, he was vouched for."

"By whom? No one here ever met him before he came from the Vatican. John, you remember him, used to have a bushy beard and long hair? He simply met the real priest before he got here and took his place. Amazing what a face and head shave can do for being recognized. Now, before you decide to raise the alarm. He's not alone. My remaining men rigged the harbor should you try to follow."

"YOU SWINE!" The admiral slapped Captain Duncan."

"Like father, like son." Duncan said smiling.

Buford was kicked in the ribs with a shout to get up just as dawn was breaking the twilight sky in the East. Blinking and wiping the sleep away from his eyes he winced in pain as his ribs were already tender from previous beatings. Gritting his teeth through the pain he stood up to take in his surroundings. The farmer and boy were also being roused by the soldiers and not any more gently than Buford received either.

"You all have an hour to empty your bowels, drink water if you'd like, say any final prayers or other rituals you may have before meeting your maker." The sergeant stated before walking away to join the soldiers cook fire and eat his breakfast.

Buford could tell that the farmer and boy got little to no sleep from the dark circles around their eyes. They also must have cried most of the night from the puffy bags underneath them. Buford could not bring himself to cry any more. He knew it was his time. Even being a deserter, he knew it was not right, he could not kill innocent people anymore. If it were only following orders it would not affect his consciousness so much. He was not going to do it any longer. He would not be remembered as a man that blindly followed orders and killed innocents, if he would be remembered at all.

Buford stepped away as far as possible with leg chains on and watered the grass. He stared back at the soldiers eating their meal and even with the abuse of the walk and the treatment he received he was not mad at them. He pitied them for just blindly following orders like he used to without question. He looked past the soldiers and their cookfire to see the rider on his horse, hooded and sitting stoically in his saddle.

At this distance Buford realized why the man looked so familiar. He wore the same coat his pa did. A black duster with wooden buckles and hip pockets. The long coat also had a tear in the left shoulder like his pa's did, but that was likely to happen to any coat due to wear from patrolling. It looked old and worn and had not been serviced for some time.

Buford still could not make out the rider's face with his hood up, but it did not matter. He was another soldier taking orders and following them blindly like everyone else here in this garrison. A breeze rolled through the little camp causing the flames of the fire to dance, but the coat of the rider remained still like the wind had not even blown by.

The gates of the garrison tore open as Moon Shadow was shoved through the parting doors. Two soldiers followed behind him and picked him up. They carried him over to the chain and added him to the line. The Major followed through shortly after and walked over to the picket line. The soldiers by the cookfire dropped their cups or bowls and raced to get in formation to meet him as he arrived.

"Sergeant. Release the farmer."

"Yes, Major Banks." The sergeant replied and hastily unshackled the farmer. The farmer stood holding the boy looking confused.

"Mr. Black, it appears that we have an opening. You will be a prisoner for 180 days with a potential for advance release. During which time you will serve as a field hand. After your sentence you will be offered conscription and the possibility of family relocation. Do you accept the offer or remain as you are?"

"Yessir, I accept" The farmer threw off the boy without hesitation. "Oh, and uh, that man who didn't give a name I believe he was a Captain, Hartford, I think." Major Banks smiled as he motioned for the guards to escort the farmer inside the garrison.

"FILTHY TRAITOR!" the boy screamed. It was the first real thing Buford had heard him say the entire time besides his name. He then looked down at Moon Shadow.

The Indian's face was bruised and swollen. It looked like they had been interrogating him all night. Buford grabbed a cup and filled it with water and brought it over for him to drink. After choking on the first few sips, he finally drank the cup.

"I am no Blackfoot," is all Moon Shadow would say. Regardless of what Buford tried to ask him.

"I know." Buford said calmly as the three of them sat quietly watching the sun rise over the next few minutes.

The sun had broken the horizon as shouts from the soldiers ordered them all to stand. Captain Miller had rejoined the outfit with additional riflemen and issued orders. The stake was removed from the ground and the three were led to the end of the garrison wall. They were unshackled and lined up with ten riflemen in front of them. The ten of them stood in a five-by-five offset formation and awaited their orders.

Beside the riflemen stood Captain Miller making final notes in his book and giving final instructions to the riflemen.

"Do any of you want a blindfold?" he asked almost sincerely.

"I would like one sir. If it's not too much trouble." The boy stated, tears beginning to well up in his eyes again.

"Very well lad. Sergeant, assist the boy." The sergeant walked over and surprisingly applied the blindfold without any insult or undo physical force. Buford was unsure if this was due to the captain's presence or if he truly did not enjoy this part of the job.

Moving back to his position on the opposing side of the formation from the Captain, Buford watched the rider sitting on his horse behind the men lower his hood. He could not believe it; it was his pa.

"Buford Stamp for the crime of desertion you are being sentenced to death by firing squad." How could his pa be here? He died years ago. This cannot be.

"Buck Boyle for the crime of being an enemy combatant you are being sentenced to death by firing squad." The rider slowly dismounted his horse and began walking around the formation.

"Moon Shadow of the Arapaho Indians, for the crimes of being an enemy combatant you are being sentenced to death by firing squad.

"Sir, they said he was Blackfoot." The sergeant stammered.

"Sergeant, we've fought many Rebs, Indians, and foreigners in this war and we both know he isn't Blackfoot. We can at least give him his dignity."

"Yessir."

Buford had lost the conversation as his pa stood next to the captain waiting. Not knowing what to do he simply looked on in disbelief.

"You were a good soldier Buford. I truly am sorry for having to do this." Captain Miller stated as he met Buford's eyes.

"Squad Ready!" The boy began to weep once more.

"Aim!" Moon Shadow stood proud and stated, "I am Arapahoe."

Luis felt the weight of the room fall on him as the curtain opened. The faces of the families of the victims held an array of emotions firmly planted on their faces ranging from sadness to anger to indifference. He accepted their blame. Someone had to pay for the crimes committed to them. To their families.

Luis observed them making comments but remained unable to perceive them unless the guard on the other side pressed his button to activate the microphone. He did not need to hear them to know what they were saying. The more outspoken families would be telling him he deserved it. He knew that was what was being said and he would not contest it.

The warden began to make a speech that sounded rehearsed for any execution and the families began taking their seats. Luis listened as Clay and the other guard continued to tighten straps, moisten his head, and prepared the gag and hood. The last two features to be added once he was able to say his last words. Words that he had been thinking about for an awfully long time.

"Does the guilty have any last words to make?" The warden stated as he finished his speech.

"Yes, warden." Luis said.

"Proceed." The warden ordered flatly as the microphone near Luis was turned on.

"Uhm...I don't want to take much time from you all, as so much has already been taken, but what I do want to say is that I'm sorry. I..."

"You're damn right you're sorry! You son of a bitch. Hey get off me. I have a right..." The mic cut off as guards restrained the man who made his way to the microphone on the other side of the glass.

Luis watched as the man was being ordered to sit and given his options. By the way the guard pointed at the door he understood and did not seem to want to move toward the microphone again. The warden nodded for Luis to continue.

"I'm sorry I could not have saved more of your families." Luis continued despite some of the puzzled faces he was receiving. "I plead guilty to everything, because someone had to be punished for the deaths of your friends and family. Whether you believe me or not, understand that I truly am sorry for all of your pain and suffering my brother caused you. Had I known what he was going to do when we walked into that store, I would have stopped him sooner. Once I heard the shooting, I found him, and he wanted me to continue killing more of the people there for a gang initiation. I could not believe what he had done and once he handed me the gun I instead shot him to protect the rest of the people there."

Luis paused for a moment holding back his tears the best he could. "You want justice, and I am gladly willing to pay for it with my life. I have accepted all responsibility for my brothers' actions as if they were my own. I willingly accept the fate that has been given to me. While I have asked for God's forgiveness, I cannot ask for yours." Luis concluded by nodding at the warden letting him know that he was finished.

"Finalize the condemned." The warden instructed as Luis was fitted with the mouth gag, the hood, and finally the electric cap. Luis heard the warden pick up the phone one last time and a moment later hung up the receiver. "No call from the governor. Gentlemen it's time."

"May God have mercy on your soul, Luis." Father David stated as he began a quiet prayer.

The room was already black for Luis as the hood did not allow him to see beyond its cloth. Clay and the other guard walked away from Luis to their positions around the room. Their steps rang in Luis' ears. Once in place the warden spoke, and Luis held his breath.

"On my command gentlemen..."

"PULL!" The crowd shouted as the guillotine plummeted downward. The blade once again finding its home. Firmly seated at the bottom of the device the crowd cheered as a soft thud resounded from retrieval basket.

"RELEASE!" The admiral shouted over to the hangman while flailing his arm upward. Duncan continued to smile as the solid ground beneath his feet gave way with a loud snap.

"FIRE!" The command was quickly silenced by the roar of the muskets firing all at once. The firing squad, Captain Smith, the sergeant, and the rider all disappeared in the cloud of smoke that brought a hail of bullets for the three facing their demise.

"INITIATE!" The warden announced. The sound of a large exhaust fan hummed on near Luis. In a split-second Luis' body stiffened as the chair came to life with sparks and buzzing. Though a shroud covered his head and hid his face it could not hide the muffled screams of agony.

Pierre felt the most excruciating pain he ever had for a mere moment, and it was gone. What remained was more of the feeling of pins and needles in a foot that was sat upon too long without the cramping. His eyes shut at the pain and the sudden drop downward. It was as if he had been hit in the gut and was unable to catch his breath. He felt hands on the sides of his head and the sensation of being lifted up off the ground. While it was quiet, the sound was muffled as if he had wax in his ears. He swore someone had just called his name. Then it came again.

"PIERRE, CAN YOU HEAR ME!" the professor shouted as Pierre opened his eyes weakly.

Reality had finally hit Pierre. He had only moments to prove his theories. He can exist apart from his body. He can take commands after being severed. He will show them all. But he was so tired.

"PIERRE, BLINK FIVE TIMES AND STICK OUT YOUR TONGUE!" commanded the professor. Pierre stared blankly for a moment then began to blink. One...two...three...four...five times. He went to stick out his tongue, but his jaw went slack and while his tongue did stick out it simply rested on his lower lip.

"Well, this is a disappointment." The professor huffed.

"Any corpse will protrude their tongue like that." Another protested.

"This proves nothing." A third shouted.

"What a waste of time." A final professor boasted. "Take that thing away executioner."

Pierre heard it all. While he may be draining rapidly of his blood and essence he still heard their comments. It infuriated him. He could not believe that they discounted everything they saw tonight between his apprentice and himself. That they dare defy the scientific evidence presented. Pierre being turned in big hands made him lose his train of thought, but not his anger.

"Uhm...Professors?" The Executioner called out. "I think you made him mad." The large man then held out Pierre's head once again to the scientists who gasped at the rage painted face that now stared at them with empty eyes.

"Well now, this is something." The professor that asked Pierre the questions stated.

"Certainly." Another agreed.

"Let me get my notebook." Another murmured as they frantically began to chatter around the head pulling out notes and calling for their assistants. Pierre could not be more pleased as his vision faded to nothingness. He pondered to himself how his work would now be leading the field with new possibilities. He was certain his assistant would carry forth his notes in his name and...wait, his assistant was now dead. Who would carry on Pierre's legacy? The darkness enveloping him seemed much more of an empty void now as he realized his work would end up costing him far much more than his life.

I:III:IV:V:IX

Duncan felt his neck snap as the rope tightened around his throat. He felt no pain, but the pressure around his neck was quickly bringing in a darkness into his eye. The world collapsed under the darkness. He was in total darkness and no sound entered his ears. Then he winked.

The noose no longer hung around his neck as he stood upon the gallows. Looking around, the world was devoid of color. No longer were there bystanders observing his death, nor a hangman standing on the gallows, nor his father walking away from where he was hung. Beyond the courtyard was darkness. No stars or moon alight in the darkness above, only more of the black veil that surrounded him.

He began to walk around and realized he no longer limped. He also now had both his eyes as he continued to survey the area noticing a much larger field of view. Movement in the darkness caught his attention as a hooded figure began to form from the darkness itself and stepped forward. Not being afraid of facing adversity he walked down the steps of the gallows to meet the figure face-to-face.

The figure stopped in the center of the courtyard where Duncan met it as it began to speak at his approach.

"William Barthalomew Baylor..."

"It's Duncan now."

"It makes no matter of precedence what you call yourself." The entity paused as it seemed to study Captain Baylor. "You have been found guilty of murdering innocents. In spite of these crimes, it has been identified that these people also murdered those around you and attempted to kill you, imprisoned, and then tortured you prior to your culling. As such you are given the right to find the path to redemption."

"And where is this path?" Duncan asked with an air of caution.

"At the bottom of the deepest and darkest pits of despair. You will be tested as you make your ascent out of the pits. Should you be successful? I will see you again. Should you fail...you will likely see me sooner for your sentencing."

"How long will these trials take?" He wondered.

"Years, perhaps decades, or longer. That depends on you." The entity uttered flatly.

"When do they begin?"

"Now." The entity spread its shadowy-robed arms exposing skeletal hands. The darkness below Duncan grew darker as it opened and he fell into its depths. No light to guide his way, no wind to judge how fast he was falling. On occasion lightning would flash in the darkness illuminating tentacled monstrosities within clouds that were an unimaginable size. As he continued to fall he started to hear screams and yells of agony coming from all directions. Odors worse than the foulest corpses he had seen in life made him retch, but nothing came up.

He was blinded by the sudden explosion of fire all around him. Flames expanded in all directions. Illuminating endless caverns and ungodly tortures as he fell through the center of a massive tunnel. Creatures of unfathomable grotesque construction armed with various crude weaponry tortured people and patrolled the caverns. The scene once again faded to darkness as he continued falling.

The unimaginable horrors he continued to see, the extreme environments he would have to endure, the gambit of emotions tore at him. He had been falling fathoms deep into the abyss until finally his feet met solid ground. In the darkness he readied himself for the challenges that lie ahead. He would have his redemption.

1:4:5:6:8-F:G:K

The deafening roar of the gunshots passed, and Buford remained standing. Smoke hung in the air. He thought to himself that the bastards missed at this close range, and he would have to endure another barrage. Through the smoke the rider, his father, emerged and approached Buford.

"Pa, how are you here? You died."

"Son, I'm not your father." The man stated. "I am simply an image that will ease your passing. Would you rather see a hooded skeleton carrying a scythe? Or perhaps some other horrid apparition?"

"Well, no, I suppose not, but shouldn't you wait until I'm dead? They're gonna need to fire a second volley so you should get out of the way."

"You're already dead Buford." The man pointed to the ground next to where Buford was standing. "You're actually the lucky one. Shot in the head and died instantly. Time, as you know it, has stopped for you. Moon Shadow will die soon, but painfully. He was shot in the lung and unless they shoot him again he'll die drowning in his own blood. The boy Buck, even longer as he was shot in both legs. Seems the firing squad didn't have the heart to shoot someone so young, but they'll have to again if they don't want him to suffer."

He looked over at the two others lying on the ground. Their faces were a mask of pain and agony frozen like the gunpowder clouds that hung in the air. Buford wondered if they had also been seeing someone like his father coming closer as death was also coming closer. Who would be their guide? Their Mother, a grandfather, a close friend? While curious he knew it was none of his business. He turned back to his father.

"So, what happens now?" Buford asked.

"Now, you move on to what lies beyond."

"And what lies beyond?"

"That depends on many things, but you were an honorable man Buford. You led an honorable life and made honorable decisions. I speculate that for you, it will be quite pleasant. However, I have been wrong before."

"That's not very reassuring."

"I do apologize, but that is not my decision to make. Come, it is time." His father walked through the smoke and grabbed the reins of his horse as Buford followed behind. As he passed by the firing squad he waved hand and a smoky portal formed in front of them. His father motioned Burford to step forward and walk through.

Stepping into the smoky ring Buford felt his body spring forward at an incredible speed. He knew he was off to be judged by some higher power. Keeping his eyes open as the world went by in a blur, he was frightened but accepted the fate that lie ahead.

1:4:7:11-XI-B:D:F:G:H

Luis' sight filled with light as the electricity surged through him. His skin tightened as it stretched and swelled from the inside constricting his restraints further. His insides were on fire as his throat let loose guttural cries of pain as he felt one of his eyes burst from its socket. Still his vision was flooded in white. His nostrils filled with the sickly-sweet scent of his own burning flesh as the electrodes seared his skin. Unable to focus on anything but the sharp sting of pain Luis became lost in the light. With one eye closed tight and the other hanging out of its socket resting on his cheek the light penetrated deep into Luis' mind. In the light Luis forgot about the pain, no longer smelling his flesh, hearing it popping like bacon, or feeling his skin tighten as it swelled.

Luis now sat erect in the chair as he did before it was turned on and began his torment. Had the first round of electrocution finished? Luis mentally checked his pants to see if he had soiled himself but appeared to be fine. He also had no sensation of needing to cough up blood or other symptoms he read about during the electrocution process. The vision of being flooded perpetually by a streaming white light was beginning to subside as if a heavy fog was lifting.

The fog revealed Luis sitting in the chair on top of himself. His body was drooping forward as much as the restraints allowed. The warden was waving over the doctor to check on Luis as it appeared the execution had finished. There was no longer sound to be heard, but as he watched the doctor move toward him, he realized he could move his arms and legs freely and stood up to move out of the way. Only then did he realize there was no longer a hood on his head, and he watched as the doctor carefully checked his smoldering body for signs of life. To Luis it was obvious he was dead, and the check was simply a redundancy for the doctor.

Turning to face the small assembly in the observation room he saw a mixture of facial expressions among the people being revealed by the receding fog being sucked out of the room. As the thin veil dissipated, he saw pale figures standing among the seated audience with a glow similar to the fog. All of them stared at Luis, a welcoming smile on their faces. It was only when he saw the little girl did he realize who was standing among the families. It was all of the victims of his brothers' actions.

"Your suffering is over Luis." The little girl stated clearly despite being behind the soundproof glass. Her voice sounded so ethereal and echoed with exuberance throughout the area. "Now, you can join us in paradise."

Luis stared in wonder. He could not believe his eyes, let alone his ears at what was unfolding before him. The faces of the family members in the room now clearer as Luis approached the glass. Most were now somber with their eyes downward regardless of their views of Luis prior to the execution. Whether it was what Luis had said or the brutal display they had just witnessed, their attitudes changed significantly. Even the man who had scolded him previously had a challenging time to keep his eyes on Luis' smoldering body. The figures shrouded in a glow began lifting their arm pointing toward a wall within the observation room.

Luis continued toward the glass as Clay walked in front of him closing the curtain to the viewing room. The curtain obstructed his view of the family members, but he could still see the glowing figures standing and pointing. Reaching forward Luis raised his own hand and watched as it passed through the curtain. He continued forward and passed through the curtain and glass with ease. Coming into the viewing room the families had begun to file out of the room through a door in the back. However, his focus was more on what the victims were pointing towards.

Following the arms Luis' gaze looked toward what was formally a wall. The wall had become a fractured hole into oblivion. The hole looked as if it were knocked away by a wrecking ball. What was left in its place was a glittering rainbow platform that led off into the distance. Luis saw a radiance on the horizon but was unsure what exactly lay at the end of road that lay before him.

As he stood there looking at the winding path before him the former victims began to file past him. They smiled at him as they passed by walking down the path. Their feet illuminated beneath them leaving residual footprints of light that slowly faded and as the people moved along the path.

Luis felt a tug at his hand. Looking down he saw the little girl holding it. "Don't worry, it only looks scary. It's so much better at the other side." She said looking up at him with innocent eyes then began to lead him down the path.

Looking back into the viewing room the exit door was closing. He was not sure if the families believed him or not, but he said what he needed. He had hoped he had reached them so there was something else on their hearts besides the hate and sadness that had built up over the years. Luis pained for them, but the weight was fading as he started taking his first steps down the illuminated path.

He hoped to see his brother one last time, but Luis knew it was not possible any longer. Keeping ahold of the little girls' hand he continued to walk down the road. They watched the horizon using the radiant light in the distance as their beacon as they walked. He held his head high for the first time in a long time.

"I'm no longer scared." He said, as a true heartwarming smile formed on his lips that had not been there for as long as he could remember.

1:4:8:11-XI-A:B:D:E:G

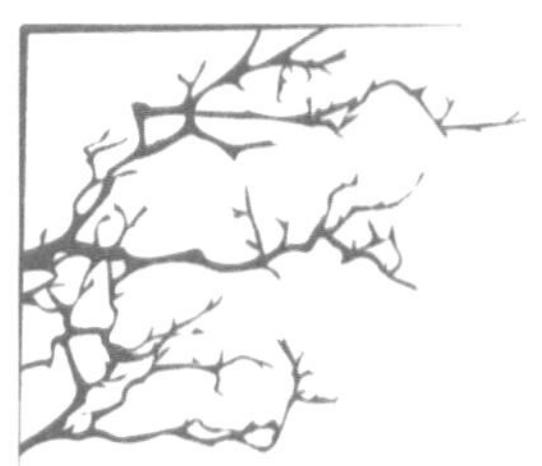

Flashes

The sound of coins hitting his aluminum can woke Harold from his chilly slumber. Although he was tucked away in a sleeping bag the sidewalk beneath him drained most of the heat out of him. Sitting up he reached forward and grabbed his can. The generosity of the city was good today as the can held several bills and not just the change that woke him. He would be able to afford a decent meal instead of having to go to the soup kitchens.

Thinking about where he would go for his meal Harold heard footsteps approaching him as he pulled the money out and began to count it.

"Whoa. Got a decent haul today." The man said with forced enthusiasm. "Let me add some more to that."

Harold looked up at the man with a grin. He reached out with his can to receive whatever the man would provide while bringing his other hand close to his chest holding on to his money. The man reminded Harold of himself when he was younger. A nice fresh cut with good line work, a smooth dark complexion with a well-trimmed thin goatee, a big over-sized coat perfect for this wintry weather, and Jordans to reflect some style. The man or rather young man, now that Harold had seen his face, smiled as he reached into his pocket revealing a few gold teeth as well. Harold felt like he was as blessed as he could be.

"Bless yo…" Harold started.

"Now hand it all over." The young man said as he produced a knife from his pocket instead of money. He crouched down to Harolds level grabbing him with his other hand and putting the knife to his throat. "Don't make me cut you."

Harold's eyes grew large at the sudden threat. It shocked him to his core, and he suddenly began to feel a tightness in his chest. His left arm fell limp as he dropped the money at his chest. His right arm dropped his can and instinctively shot over to grab his left shoulder causing the young man's knife to slice Harold's throat as his body seized up. Harold felt the sharp pain of the knifepoint cutting into his neck, unable to do anything for himself as the pain in his chest began to crush him. The young man also shocked at what had happened dropped his knife and grabbed what money he could in Harold's lap, ignoring the overturned can, and ran.

"Hey stop!" A voice shouted from across the street. Rushing footsteps made their way over to Harold. "Holy crap buddy. Hold on, I'll call for help." Dialing 911 the new man pulled off his scarf and put it Harold's neck. As he lie on his back clutching his shoulder Harold began to lose consciousness.

The day was sunny and hot. Harold was playing on the playground with his friends. They ran all over the grounds, going down the slides, swinging on the tires, bouncing on the see-saws, and playing tag. They were going wild on their break from the classroom. Their teachers watched from the entrance to the school shouting at students who were getting too rough. Harold and his friends played even harder when they heard words of encouragement as the teachers began to shout "Run!"

Only when they heard the all-too-familiar sounds of gunfire did Harold and the rest of the children react. Many ran to get behind something, some tried to get inside the school, others simply jumped to the ground. The shots lasted only a moment as the sound of screeching tires peeling away down the street revealed the threat was gone. Immediately, the teachers told the students to move inside. Harold reached over to help his friend Lamar, who laid on the ground next to him. Harold's hand felt wet and he saw blood on his hand as he looked down at it. Sitting there frozen in shock, a teacher came and grabbed him by the shoulder.

"Harold, are you okay?"

"Hey man, are you okay?" A man looking down on Harold asked with his hands pressed down on his chest. "Stay with me. Help is on the way."

Harold had his eyes barely open. He could not manage any words or even raise his hands. The cold cement below him radiated through his body as he began to shiver violently.

The pain in his chest remained and seemed to be more prevalent now. The pain radiated into his ribs and his breathing was beginning to be difficult. Lacking efficient oxygen Harold felt his eyes closing and losing consciousness once again.

"Just hang on buddy. Help is on the way..."

"...Help is on the way, son." Harold told the young man. Regardless of the situation he did not want the kid to die. He was only protecting himself from the kid making an unwise decision. The young man had not expected Harold to be so quick to respond to the robbery. Harold frequented this particular shop before and after his shift most days. Today happened to be at the end of his shift and being a detective, he was in plain clothes and already inside shopping, not driving a standard police cruiser. If he had only dropped the gun like Harold instructed, he would not be on the ground in a pool of his own blood with Harold applying pressure to the wound.

Harold knew the situation was not going to turn out in this kids favor, but he planned on doing his best to ensure he saw tomorrow. When the paramedics arrived they began to work on him as Harold pulled personal effects to make a report with the other officers that arrived on scene. Looking at his ID a Robert Davis only 20 years old. Harold began to fill out the report when he received a text.

"Where are you?"

Looking over the text Harold replied: "*Finishing up some paperwork and I'll be on the way.*"

"*Good. You can finally meet my boyfriend.*"

"*Lol. Who's that?*"

"*Bobby D! How many times do I have to tell you? Now get home!*"

"*Okay sweetie.*"

Harold put away the phone to finish his report. Digging through the evidence bag he annotated the revolver, cell phone, set of house keys, set of car keys, a wallet with a debit card, gym membership, $13 cash, and photo strip. Setting everything aside he glanced back at the photo and saw it was a set of pictures from a photo booth of Robert Davis and his daughter. He sighed as he tucked the evidence away as this was not how he intended on meeting the young man. He finished his report, turning in his gun as procedure dictated, and checked in with the paramedics.

"How's the kid doing?

"He didn't make it. Tried for nearly fifteen minutes to bring him back." Noticing the disappointment on Harold's face the medic added, "Don't beat yourself up about it. You did your best."

"Yeah." Harold turned and got in his car. Once he got on the road and started driving home he received another text from his daughter.

"*Where are you?*"

"*I'm almost there...*"

"We're almost there buddy." A paramedic said to Harold with assurance. The pain in his chest persisted and it was still difficult to breath, but he could now feel that he was strapped to a gurney and had a bag assisting him in breathing. The light from the ceiling of the ambulance was blinding and his eyes would barely open. He was no longer freezing lying on the gurney as it appeared to be heated.

The back of the ambulance was crowded. The two paramedics worked on him while a third person sat and kept an eye on him. He did not recognize the woman, but she must have been one of the people that helped him on the street. The police would likely want a statement from her once they arrived at the hospital so that was quite considerate of her Harold thought. He did his best to stay conscious and alert, but the pain in his chest and the bumping of the vehicle was swiftly bringing him back to unconsciousness.

"I don't think so, we are not going to lose you." The paramedic shouted.

"I don't want to lose you." Harold's daughter said crying.

"Oh sweetie, you're not going to lose me. Your mom and I just can't deal with each other any longer. It is not your fault. Besides, you have your own family to worry about." Harold hoped she would not smell the alcohol on his breath. Even though he could no longer bear to be with his wife, it did not mean he was not hurting. Since he had retired from the force money had been tight and finding work was difficult. It seemed no one wanted to hire an aging police officer.

"I've been through worse situations than this. "

"Okay dad. I know you won't tell me if you're struggling. Just, don't give up."

"Don't give up." Was all Harold heard amidst the chaos of beeping machines. It resembled a female's voice, but nothing was visible through the light. Hands touched him, a needle pierced his hand, air was forced into his lungs, and the persistent pain constricting his chest continued to cause him agony every waking moment. A steady beeping in the room quickly started to become erratic until the tone leveled out as the pain in his chest became unbearable.

"Clear!" Another voice yelled as Harold felt a massive jolt surged though his chest. His body seized as the voltage coursed through him and raised him up off the table he was laying on. The beeping in the room resumed as the pain in his chest had been numbed by the shock. The beeps once again coalesced into a solid tone as his chest began to tighten once again. The light in his eyes began to fade. "Clear!" once again rung in Harold's ears as another surge powered through his chest causing him to seize as light filled his vision only for a moment.

"Clear out!" The slum lord said to Harold.

"But my stuff is still inside."

"That's not my problem." You're three months behind. Unless you have it, all of that is collateral to pay for the past due rent. Now beat it."

Harold thought about pushing past the man, but the hulking maintenance man, if that's what you could call him, more like hired muscle, who was changing his locks kept his hand near the tool bag. It seemed he knew what Harold was thinking and kept his eye on him as he paused his work on the lock. Noting the change in the man's behavior Harold decided to turn away and leave the apartment.

It had been three days since his car was repossessed and now his home. If he could call it that. The small one-bedroom apartment was no bigger than a glorified walk-in closet for all the space he had. At least it provided a roof over his head. Now he had nothing and no idea of what he was going to do.

Harold learned quickly that it did not matter if he was homeless or not. He evidently carried himself too proudly at first and found himself being robbed of what little money he did have left. He went to the shelters in the beginning, but after his daughter had shown up looking for him, he stopped going due to his shame and not wanting her to see him as he now was. Broken, beaten, and in shambles. His downward spiral was a slow and insidious descent into the shadows of his own challenges and adversities. It began slow with inconspicuous setbacks that, over time, snowballed into a cascade of difficulties. He turned to panhandling for money and found that anything he made was wasted on alcohol. Soon he became a shell of the man he once was on the streets he once patrolled.

The next several years were a blur to Harold. As the spiral deepened, his physical health also began to suffer. Neglected self-care, coupled with the repeated substance abuse, took a hit on his vitality. The vibrance that once defined him was replaced by weariness, visible in his demeanor and the lines etched on his face. Ashamed of the life he now lived the alcohol numbed the pain and so he lingered in the streets.

The sound of coins hitting his aluminum can woke Harold from his chilly slumber...

Harold gasped as he leapt up from where he was lying in the dark room. Looking around he could not make out anything in the darkness save a single hanging light that hung outside double doors illuminating the space around it. As his eyes adjusted the light that bled into the room revealed that it was a large room with several tables.

"Good, you're awake." A woman's voice called out to him from the darkness behind him.

"Who's there?" He demanded. "Where am I?"

"It's ok Harold. You're safe. Let me put on some lights." She suddenly clapped her hands causing the fluorescent hanging lights scattered throughout the room to burst to life.

Harold winced at the sudden radiance. Taking in the surroundings he realized that he was in a sterile medical room. The were stainless steel tables lined in a row with instrument carts parked at the head of most tables. Lab coats hung on a rack next to the double doors. As he looked at the wall he held his breath.

"Yes, Harold. This is the morgue." The voice caused him to turn away from the wall. Harold gazed upon a beautiful woman, with pale skin, flowing black hair that fell below her waist dressed in a skintight black knee length dress that opened up to flowing tassels at the elbows and knees. She wore no shoes or jewelry that he could see. On the instrument table next to her rested an unlit lantern and ebony cane.

"Why am I here? I saw the doctors. They were saving me."

"Unfortunately, they did all they could Harold, but it wasn't enough."

"So, what now? You take me to Hell for my sins?"

"Hell? Why would I do that Harold?"

"From all the bad in my life. I just saw my life flash before my eyes and it's all bad. Why shouldn't I go there?"

"Harold, you saw those memories, because that is what is always on your mind. What haunts you? That is not who you are. Who you were. Who this man was." She pointed over to a steel table where a body was covered with a sheet.

Harold looked at the sheet covered body and walked over. He moved his hand down to lift the sheet then stopped himself. He knew it was his body. He did not need further proof that he was dead. The woman, he realized, had been standing at the head of this table the whole time. He turned back toward her.

"Then what kind of man am I? Look at me. I'm in rags, I'm filthy, and if I could smell myself, I'm sure it would be quite foul."

"Let me show you Harold." She reached her hand up toward Harold's head. He flinched at her hand and grabbed her wrist. "I assure you; I am only giving you what you ask." He released her wrist, which felt ice cold, and allowed her to touch his face. Her hand was colder than her wrist and he was instantly flooded with memories.

On the playground Harold only remembered running around playing. When the shots began flying in their direction, he led several of his classmates to safety in the playground. When the shooting had stopped, and a teacher came to get him. He was helping Lamar who had been shot in his leg. With his quick thinking he possibly saved the lives of many of his classmates without realizing it.

When the officers arrived, he remembered more than he thought about the car and with his confidence the other students were able to give enough of a description to track down the car and the shooters. His uncle being on the force told him he was proud of him and that he would make a great police officer one day. It was that day that he decided that was what he was going to do when he grew up.

He was back in the memory when he shot his daughter's boyfriend. At dinner he told her the news of what had happened and as predicted she reacted horribly. She blamed her father. He tried to console her, but it was no use. Several hours later she came crashing into her parents' bedroom crying even more and apologizing for being upset. She could not get the words out and turned on the tv. The news reported on the shooting and were reporting that he was connected to three other murders of females throughout the area.

The phone rang as they were consoling their daughter. Harold's superior called to congratulate him on stopping the man from becoming the next serial killer.

"Captain Wright, what can I do for you?"

"Just wanted to call and congratulate you Harold."

"For what sir?"

"It seems Robert Davis was not just simply dating your daughter. He was gathering information on your whole family. It's likely he knew you'd be at the market, just not sure at what time and you got the drop on him. From the evidence we gathered at his apartment he was likely planning on increasing his body count and becoming our next serial killer."

"I see sir."

"Don't you worry about a thing Harold. We'll see you commended for this. The department definitely holds you in high regard."

"Thank you sir."

Harold was back with his daughter amid a terrible divorce after a successful career as an officer. She pleaded with him to stay, but ultimately had to leave. She did not want to lose him and as he left he told her, "Don't you worry about me. Besides, you are still going to back to college with what I've got left. I'll always take care of you baby girl."

Regardless of the financial hardship Harold suffered he made sure his daughter was taken care of despite not being there physically. He moved into his crummy apartment and drove a car that only worked when it wanted to. He still managed until he was evicted after a couple of years when he could no longer make payments on both the school loans and his apartment and car. He decided paying off the school debt was the priority.

Living on the streets may have been a haze, but Harold still served those that needed more than he. He consistently gave his food to others in his homeless community, offered a helping hand to drivers who had broken down, and protected those less fortunate when he could. No one expected a bum to stop a purse snatcher, a potential back-alley rape, or even stop a potential robbery or arson if he was able.

While he was ashamed of his lifestyle and did not want his daughter to find him that did not stop him from visiting her in his own way. He frequently visited her family apartment and stood outside and watched over them. He even saved his granddaughter from being hit by a car when her ball rolled into the road. His daughter had missed the incident but heard the car honk. She berated him as she only saw him holding her little girl, he put her down and ran off before she found out who he was.

Harold jolted backwards as he snapped back to the present. The cold washing over his head was slowly dissipating. He breathed rapidly trying to catch his breath. Composing himself he stood unsure of what exactly had happened. He looked at the woman who was lowering her arm and was reaching down at the tray to pick up the lantern and cane.

"I told you Harold, who you saw first was not who you are. Who you just saw is who you are. You are all full of flaws, but those flaws do not define you. What you do despite those flaws is what truly defines you."

"But nobody knows what I've done, and now that I'm gone there won't be anyone to care about what I was anyhow. I'll be forgotten."

"That is true Harold. In time we are all forgotten. However, we still have a lasting impact. Lamar has never forgotten that you saved his life. Should you have reached out to him when you were in a bad place, he would have helped you out without hesitation. Your daughter has a successful career and a loving family due to your sacrifice and she will always cherish your support. Only after calming down from when you saved her little girl did she realize it was you and she waits by her window nightly for you to come by again. The countless people in the homeless community praise you for your selflessness, the random strangers you've helped constantly think back to you helping them and some have even tried looking for you to give you a reward. You are honored in the police force for your service and your dedication is something many officers aspire to achieve. Even the people who interacted with you tonight are affected by your influence. The man who called 911, the man who started CPR, the medics in the ambulance, the doctors that tried to save your life and even the man who stabbed you. All are affected by the events of today and by your actions."

"All I did was get stabbed and have a heart attack. And what does the man that stabbed me have to do with anything, but ruin my life?"

"He gets identified by the man that called 911. He goes to jail and is killed in a prison riot. He is an organ donor. His liver saves your granddaughters life."

"So, you're saying if this hadn't happened, my granddaughter would die?"

"Not necessarily, but it is likely. So, you see. You are important regardless of life or death, whether remembered or forgotten."

"Alright, so what happens now?"

"That choice is yours. We have a destination, but the path is yours to choose. Would you like to take the stairs, the road, or the river?"

As she spoke three of the walls broke away. One revealed a shimmering path that led off into the distance. Another had a luminescent stairwell that winded upward disappearing upon its many twists and turns. The last led to a dark river illuminated from within as streaks of light moved in the direction of the flow. A boat docked at the edge of the room creaked as the water rocked it up and down.

"Where do they all lead?" Harold asked looking on in wonder.

"To your next journey. Come, we have much to discuss during your transition." The lantern she held began to glow a green light as the fluorescent lights blinked out. Lifting her arm with the cane in it she presented it to Harold.

Taking her arm, he thought about the paths ahead of him within the radiance of the eerie green light. Unsure of where he was headed, he choked down his fear, decided, and moved forward. He had been in worse situations than this.

1:4-XI-B:C:E:G:H:I:K

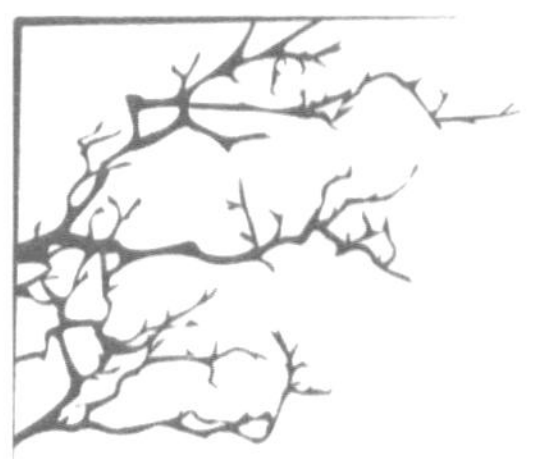

Martyr

The sounds of sirens began to fill the air in the distance. The threats had been called in and the authorities would now begin evacuating the area. Connor did not want to kill innocent people to get the message across of their group's dissatisfaction with the country's leaders and their so-called peace agreements. However, he did not have to worry about that as they have received their threats and the police would be here to ensure the area was clear.

Connor continued to watch over the plaza where they had parked the large car bomb. It was void of people as were the commercial offices due to the weekend work hours. Despite the lack of casualties from this bomb the collateral damage to the area will deal a significant blow to their opposition. After his scan he began radio checks of his personnel.

"We are all set here. Once you let me know we're good I'll start the timer."

"All set East side."

"All set North side."

"All set West si...hold on."

"What is wrong West?" Connor shouted into the radio.

"People are moving into the area. The idiot police are evacuating the wrong area."

"How long until they get here?"

"They'll be in the area within 10 minutes.

"Shit. We don't have another opportunity. We have to go." Connor told them. "Do what you can to deter them from the area. I'm setting the timer for five minutes."

Connor pulled out his remote and set the timer. Looking out onto his view of the quarter he saw no one in the plaza yet. He still had time and pressed the activation button.

"All sectors evacuate the area and rendezvous at the designated location and time." Connor began his descent down the stairwell. His radio crackled but nothing coherent came through due to the stairwell. He reached the ground level and exited the back of the building and put on his worker's reflective vest. All the others should be doing the same.

More crackling came over the radio. "...you copy?"

"I did not copy. Say again." Connor replied.

"This is North, we now have people moving quickly in from this direction."

"West! What is going on?"

"Someone in the police must have mentioned the bomb and it spread like wildfire. Everyone is panicking. That plaza is going to be full by the time it happens."

"Do what you can to turn those people around. I'll work it from the plaza."

"Are you crazy? That's ground zero!"

"Godspeed lads. Godspeed."

Connor turned off his radio and put it in his pack. Placing his pack on the ground he reached in and grabbed his AK-47 with folded stock. Dropping the bag to the ground he moved to the front of the building and into the plaza. As the street opened up to the sprawling expanse of commercial buildings lining either side of the open square Connor could see people start pouring into the area from the North and West. Knowing his time was short he acted without hesitation and began shooting into the air. The people seeing him running towards them began shouting and screaming in terror as they saw a gunman shooting in their direction. The crowds began to disperse in the direction they were coming from with a few diving into alleys and behind cover to hide from the shooter.

The North side had been diverted when Connor turned to have the people coming in from the west do the same instead of trying to hide. As people began seeing the shooter coming in their direction shouts to run began to echo through the crowd. He saw the crowds turning as he continued to fire in the air. Ditching the gun in a post box Connor began to sprint as fast as he could from the area.

BOOM

The blast from the bomb was unlike anything Connor had ever experienced. He felt the blast hit him and tear him apart. He felt his body sear with the heat of it. In an instant he was upright and running and the next he was lying on his back facing the sky. In the shock he felt no pain as he looked down and saw the lower half of his body missing as well as his left arm and most of his right. His head fell backward onto the ground, and he watched as the sky was consumed by the fire and smoke from the bomb. He heard screaming all around him from the people who were unable to get away. The buildings were crumbling under their own weight due to the damaged supports and foundations. The building looming over Connor made an ungodly groan as it came crashing down on top of him casting him in darkness.

The darkness erupted into flames, he could feel his body and limbs burning. Screaming out in pain he looked down and saw his body burning as the world around him had turned to fire and ash. Getting upright he found himself in the middle of an endless lake of fire. All around the lake he saw people in various stages of torment.

The captives were in cages, hanging by chains, or contorted in unimaginable positions within unspeakable torture devices. Others were being flayed, whipped, beaten, and more while being seared by the flames of the lake. Each of the people he saw were paired with a devil, demon, or beast of all manner of grotesqueness. Everywhere he looked he saw horns and spikes, slime and spittle, claws and teeth, wings, and tails.

Fear gripped as the lake in front of Connor began to bubble up. Out of the smoke above him two chains propelled out and shackled onto his wrists lifting him just above the lake. The bubble of molten fire grew as tall as Connor and burst spraying him and searing his flesh. He screamed out in pain as the molten fire carved paths down his body causing him to squeeze his eyes shut.

"OPEN YOUR EYES!" A guttural unnatural voice shouted.

Connor opened them hesitantly. A dark beast with yellow eyes and a multi-horned head stood before him. It's face a cross between a lizard and bird and its body a boney husk barely covered in flesh and every inch covered in barbs. It carried a multi-strapped whip tipped with hooks in one of its three clawed hands and lifted it as the creature began to speak.

"FILTH! YOU ARE HEREBY SENTENCED TO AN ETERNITY OF TORMENT FOR THE SINS OF THE FLESH."

"But I saved those people. There must be a mistake." Connor pleaded with fear in his eyes.

"*INSOLENT WHELP! TWENTY-NINE PEOPLE WERE SLAIN IN THE BLAST. ANOTHER TWO HUNDRED INJURED. YOU CALL THAT A MISTAKE? DO YOU SEE YOURSESLF A MARTYR FOR YOUR CAUSE SIMPLY BECAUSE YOU DIED ATTEMPTING TO RIGHT A WRONG?*"

"No, I..."

"*SILENCE! BEING OF CHRISTIAN FAITH, AND CATHOLIC NO DOUBT, YOU SHOULD KNOW BETTER THAN MOST THAT NO LAW IS ABOVE THAT OF YOUR LORD. AND YET YOU CAUSE SUCH DESTRUCTION IN ORDER TO PERSUADE OTHERS ONE WAY OR ANOTHER.*"

Connor protested only a moment longer then allowed himself to go limp. He knew what he had done was wrong. Nothing he ever did could ever prepare him for what now lay before him.

"*IT'S GOOD YOU UNDERSTAND YOUR PLACE, BUT IT WILL DO YOU NO GOOD. SHALL WE BEGIN?*" The demon laughed as it raised the whip.

The beast made a turning motion with its open claw causing the chains to turn Connor around and face away from it. The first slap of the whip on his back caused him to gasp in pain. It was not until the beast ripped the hooks, connected to the lashings, which tore his flesh that he let out the first of many screams.

His screams were lost within the endless chorus that echoed above the molten lake. Connor, among countless others, felt nothing but sorrow as the heat of the molten lake seared his flesh after every strike. His eyes forced open with his tears drying up as soon as they formed, his mouth parched never to be quenched again, and every inch of his body writhed in pain. He could do nothing but take the eternal torment. With eyes pried open he watched as others received their torment and even more arrived to begin their anguish.

1:8:11-VIII-B:F:G:H

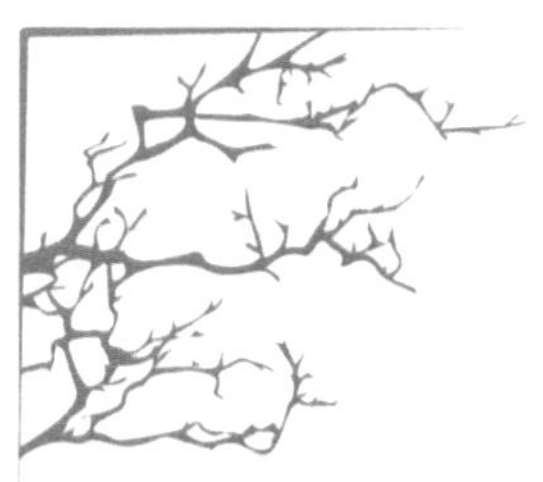

Wraith

Riley awoke in darkness. Her body bound upright to some metal slab. Her wrists and ankles fastened to the metal by leather straps tightened to the point that they cut into her. Her head was also strapped down tightly, unable to turn. She tried to scream but was suppressed with a leather strap and ball gag. Her jaw was strained by the tightness of the strap and extended time her jaw must have been opened. She felt cold and realized she was naked as well. The feeling of helplessness and dread washed over her as she wondered how this happened.

As she began to sense more of her body she felt that she had something wrapped around her left arm. Her genitals were sore as well as her back and it felt like her face was swollen. She could not understand what had happened or what she did to deserve to be in this situation. Tears began to stream down her face.

The sound of a large metal latch opening caused her to catch her breath. A heavy looking door swung outward letting light spill into the room. Riley could only use her eyes to look around. As the door was fully opened a tall dark figure entered and stood menacingly in the shadows a moment before reaching over to switch on the lights in the room. After switching on the lights, he closed the door and latched it.

Riley took in the room as the man was closing the door in a desperate attempt to map out the room in case she could get loose. The room was small and confined and stank of mildew. The stone walls sweat, and a drain was located on the floor. A television was propped up a few feet in front of her. The wall next to it had a large corkboard with missing person posters and newspaper articles of missing men and women, found bodies, and unsolved murders pinned to it as a sort of sick shrine.

The rest of the room was barren save the metal table onto which she was strapped. Her arm had an IV in it with a smaller table next to her with additional IV's and various drug vials. Her breath caught as she spotted a surgical cart on the other side with a variety of cutting instruments used by doctors. She started to breath rapidly thinking about their use.

"Don't get ahead of yourself dear." The man's voice said as he grabbed hold of her chin. Her eyes darted to meet his as she let out a muffled yelp. His face was covered by a nondescript emotionless red mask. All she could see was his dead blue eyes behind the mask and his brown hair jutting up from behind it. He was shirtless but wore a personalized black apron that read *'Don't worry I can do this. I watched a YouTube video. -Chef Derick.'* He was muscular and she knew she would not be able to overpower him.

"You know Riley, we've had such a fun time. I almost don't want to do this." He grabbed her breast and slightly lifted his mask as he licked the side of her face. As she whimpered he stopped and looked down at her groin. He rubbed his hand up her inner thigh and up to her sensitive areas that ached when he roughly touched them. After groping her for a second he brought his hand up in between their faces covered in blood.

"I suppose I got a little rough. Oh, that's right you don't remember. Don't worry I recorded it for you." Laughing he wiped his hand off on her face and breasts as she winced and yelped. Turning he pulled out a remote from his pants pocket and switched on the tv and started a video. On the screen Riley was strapped into some sexual device that allowed him to manipulate her position. She was unconscious in the device, but it did not matter as it allowed him to do whatever he desired. She closed her eyes when she saw him begin to sodomize her. He wore the mask in the video as well, so she still had no idea who he was.

"You don't want to watch? But that's one of my favorite parts. You take those slaps to the backside and your face like a good girl. You were so into it." He joyfully stepped around the room prepping his instruments.

"LOOK AT ME!" Riley opened her eyes to him holding a syringe. "Here's your cocktail. Don't worry this one won't put you to sleep. I want you to be awake for the next part."

He injected the drug into her IV and she immediately started to feel the effects of it. Her body started to get warm as the drug moved through her veins. As she felt her face getting warm her captor put devices in her eyes to keep them from closing. She could feel her body start going limp.

"It's fast isn't it. Let's give it a check." He raised a scalpel up as he grabbed onto one of her nipples. He swiftly cut it off, but the pain was excruciating. Riley screamed behind the gag. Unable to blink only increased her screams as he lifted it up for her to see. She knew if his lips were exposed they would be curled into a sinister smile, instead it was hiding behind that emotionless mask.

"I guess it's not completely set in yet. I'll give you a couple more minutes. I don't want you passing out on me."

The pain quickly began to subside. Her breathing slowed as the pain faded. Riley knew that she would die here and soon. The fact that he was forcing her to watch him rape and sodomize her as he tortured her no longer caused her to fear. The fear of the unknown was gone now that reality was brought to light. She was now filled with anger. Anger that she had not done anything. Anger that she was forced to watch and unable to do anything. Anger that she did not know who he was.

"Ahhh. Now where were we?" He turned back from the tv and zipped up his pants. "I'm not gonna lie Riley, you're probably not gonna like this next part. Me on the other hand? I'm gonna to love it."

The man began cutting and slicing into her. Unsure of what he gave her she could not feel anything but remained awake through it all. He mutilated her genitals, removed her breasts, her lips, some of her teeth, an ear, flayed open her abdomen and much more. He was careful not to nick or cut anything vital. He placed everything in a bucket that was underneath the table and sprayed down the floor on occasion with a hose that hung on the wall behind her.

After what was an eternity of torture he leaned in for what seemed to be a kiss with the mask. In her weakened state she still raged at his atrocities knowing he had done this countless other times from the articles on the wall. As he leaned back he raised the scalpel to her neck and sliced it. Severing her carotid artery Riley was quickly losing consciousness. The last thing she saw was his cold dead eyes inches from her face as everything went black.

Screaming and violently flailing her arms Riley awoke in a dark room. While there appeared to be no light she was able to see that this was the room where she was just tortured. She realized that her scream was silent and tried to do it again with nothing forming. In the dark room light still radiated from everywhere and nowhere and gave everything a soft glow. She could see in this darkness. The tv still sat against the far wall in front of the table, articles were still pinned to the corkboard, the metal table bordered by the instrument table and the drugs and IV table were still there. The bucket placed beneath the table and the hose on the wall behind the table. One detail she had not known before was that a doorway to another room was also behind the table.

She wandered into the room and realized it was where he had assaulted her. Slightly larger than the other room with several cameras set up around the contraption. There was a small cabinet against the wall and a bed on wheels that looked like it was moved back and forth in front of the contraption.

Disgusted by the device Riley walked back into the torture room knowing that she was dead and that she must be some sort of lingering spirit. The table appeared to still hold her lifeless body as she quickly looked away from it. He apparently had not had time to dispose of her yet. She wanted to find out where she was at and walked over to the door not wanting to see the horror of what her body looked like. As she went to grab the latch she could not grasp it to turn it. Realizing she phased right through the latch she proceeded to walk through the door. On the other side she saw a corridor with stairs leading up, but she also saw the man in the mask coming in her direction. Panicked, she went back inside the room.

Riley thought it was dumb that she instinctively went to hide. He obviously did not see her as he did not react. Instead of hiding she decided to see what he would do with her body and try to do something with the information. She was here so she might as well do what she could to stop him.

The door began to swing open, and light filtered in. As the man stepped in and turned on the light Riley realized that it was not her body. A new woman had been abducted, assaulted, and was about to be tortured and murdered.

"WAKE UP!" The man shouted as he slapped the woman.

A whimper came from the woman as she slowly opened her eyes and started to scream through the gag as reality began to set in on her.

"Oh Angela, don't be like that. We're gonna have so much fun together. I mean we already have. Don't you remember?" He turned to the television and turned it on to show her what he had done to her in the other room. Terror filled Angela's eyes. She scanned the room and saw the posters and news articles and screamed louder.

"Oh, that's right, your poster got out so much faster than most. You must be popular. Though, I must say, that is not a good photo of you. Not like the video I took. You look so precious in mine." Laughing he pulled off the missing poster and posed with it next to her then by the television before pinning it back up. Riley looked at it and saw the dates then saw the date of her article when they found her body. She had been dead for over four months. She was enraged seeing the article and remembered what had happened to her. What he had done to her. What he was about to do to Angela. She was so angry she swiped at the article on the board causing the pin to come out and the paper to fall to the ground.

As the article fell to the ground the man looked over. He was about to inject Angela with the same cocktail he did to Riley. Setting down the syringe he walked over and picked up the article and pinned it back onto the board.

"Now, there was girl who knew how to have a fun time, Angela. You'd do well to learn from Riley. Oh wait, she's dead. Well, maybe you can meet up when we're finished. You know birds of a feather and all that." He laughed to himself.

Riley fumed at every word he said. As he moved back to the table she walked past him and tried to pick up the syringe. Her hand passed through as he grabbed it and picked it up.

"Time for your cocktail, Angela." He reached for the IV line and went to insert the syringe as Riley swiped at it again. This time the syringe fell from his hand and broke on the floor.

"What the hell? Damn gloves. No worries sweetheart I've got more supplies in the other room. Be right back. Don't go anywhere."

The man walked off into the other room to the cabinet in the corner to retrieve another syringe. Riley followed him in there and moved toward the contraption in the center of the room. As the man rifled through the drawers she thought about what he did to her here. What he had to all the others and to Angela that was now playing on the tv. She could not contain herself any longer and let loose another silent scream of rage and attacked the device. A support beam that would normally shackle wrists fell forward with a loud bang.

"Holy shit." The man jumped as he turned away from the cabinet with syringe in hand. "Must have forgot to replace the locking bolt." Shaking off the incident he walked back into the smaller room. Picking up the drug vial he inserted the syringe to begin filling it.

Riley had followed him back into the small and slapped the vial to the ground smashing it. Making the dead eyes behind the mask widen in shock.

"What is going on?" Dropping the syringe, he grabbed a scalpel from the instrument table and held it up in front of himself. He slashed at the air in an attempt to attack the unseen force berating him. "Who are you? What do you want?"

Riley smiled as the man's sense of calm seemed to be fading as she began to gain a sense of control over her newly found abilities. She pushed him backwards into the television breaking the screen. He fell to the ground dropping the scalpel and holding the back of his head as she caused the tv to fall onto him. The glass from the screen cut into his arms and head and caused him to bleed from several places. Pushing the tv off himself, he struggled to get to the door and pull himself up.

"I don't know what this is, but I'll be back." He growled as he unlatched the door and began to swing it open. Not waiting for it to be fully open he took a step out. Riley slammed the door shut with ease causing the man's ankle to shatter and hit his face with it knocking him to the ground once more. The door remained open, but his shattered leg remained in the doorway unable to break free from the weight of the door.

The man lay sprawled out on his back groaning, his corny apron laying off to his side as the strap around his back had come undone. Riley stood over him looking down at the mask that hid his face. She reached forward and ripped it off casting it aside. He gasped in terror.

She stood there looking at a somewhat familiar face. She barely knew the man and could not remember his name. She only knew him from the mobile vet clinic she would take her cat to once in a while for her shots and a checkup. She did not remember if he was a vet or an assistant.

No wonder he had not been caught. He could select his victims at random hold them for a while and dump the bodies nowhere near where he abducted them with solid alibis and have access to all the drugs he needed. He would never get caught if he stayed under the radar. Riley figured if he ever got close to being caught the person would simply end up disappearing.

Looking down at the man he seemed unsure of what to do. He tried to get up but was held down by the unseen force that Riley was now easily controlling. She saw the scalpel on the floor that she knocked out of his hand earlier and picked it up. In his eyes it began to float towards him, and they grew wide with fear as it approached his throat.

"No, please..." The man began to plead as she sliced into his neck the same way he did in the end. While she wanted to torture him, she wanted him dead more. She sat on his chest as he began to bleed out and choke on his own blood. His eyes then changed from fear of death to bewilderment as he now was able to see her.

"Ri..Ril..ey?" He sputtered as his eyes started to roll back into his head. She just stared at him smiling as she watched him realize his own sins had come to reap him. Once the life had left him she got up and moved towards the table. Angela was wide-eyed after witnessing the entire experience. The floating scalpel probably did not help the situation either.

Knowing it would likely scare her more Riley quickly dropped the scalpel and released Angela's restraints. Angela took off the ball gag herself and worked the knots out of her jaw. She was weak, not having eaten for an unknown number of days and only having an IV provide her hydration, but she was able to slowly stepped down from the table.

Walking toward the door she struggled to push it open, but Riley provided her some aid. The sudden ease of the door moving scared her, but Angela stopped and looked back before exiting the small room of hell.

"Thank you, Riley." She said weakly and made her way out of the room and into her freedom.

A portal of light opened in the upper corner of the room. She heard beautiful music and voices calling to her that soothed her. Sounds that made her feel at peace. She began floating up and being welcomed into the bliss of it all. It was all so beautiful, and she was enamored by it. As she floated across the room Riley's eyes caught the board with all the articles and reports and all the bliss and warmth faded from her. She was once again filled with a cold rage. Looking at the portal as she forced her feet down and planted herself firmly to the ground. Riley shouted into the light as the portal swirled to a close.

"I'M NOT DONE!"

1:4:11-II:VI:XI-A:B:G

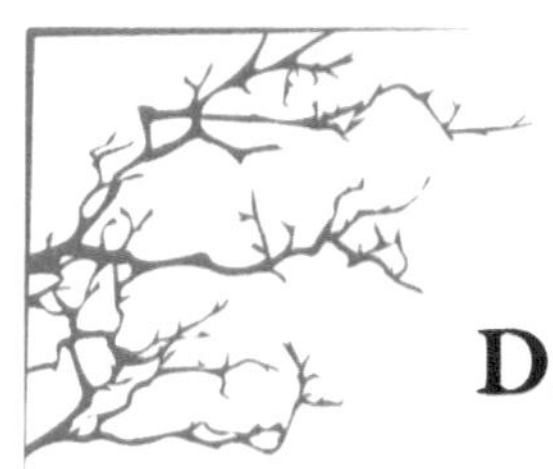

Dreaming of Adventure

Tymor, Valrick, Piers, and Magh were an inseparable group. They had been together for many seasons and grown very fond of one another since their chance meeting in a tavern in some no name village in the middle of nowhere. It would seem fate had brought them together and fate kept them together. These four unlikely companions with seemingly nothing in common have learned to coexist in a world where death could be around the next corner, over the next hill, or even occur while you slept.

The campsite was alive with activity after the recent raid of an evil witch's coven. The four were doing various tasks in setting things up for the evening. None seemed to be moving with much haste which always brought out the worst in Tymor.

"Let's go everyone. Sunset is less than an hour and we still need to eat." Tymor stated.

"Then quit barking orders and start helping out." Piers retorted.

"If ye'd stay on task instead of trying to steal more than yer fair share every five seconds I wouldn't have ta keep saying something."

"Oh, cut it out you two." Valrick interrupted. "We're done here. I'll get the fire going. Magh isn't it your turn to cook?"

"Why? Because I'm the only woman?" She snorted.

"Uhm, no. Because it's your turn in the rotation."

"Uh...oh."

Magh began preparing the food as Val started the fire. Tymor pulled a pack from his horse and brought it over to the fire as Piers tuned up his lyre and kicked a log over to sit on. They all settled in around the fire picking off pieces of meat from the carcass cooking above it as the juices fell into the coals. Tymor began digging through the bag pulling out various treasures from the coven's defeat.

"Wasn't a large haul this time. I expect our real reward that we get from the town magistrate will even it all out once we arrive tomorrow." Tymor explained.

"Weren't that strong either." Magh sighed.

"That was a little disappointing." Piers agreed, pausing on his lyre to comment then began strumming once more.

"Not that you'll need any Tymor. You'll just donate it to the temple." Val prodded.

"What I do with my spoils are of my concern, Val. What you do with yours are yours. Besides you're the one to talk."

"What are you talking about?"

"Back in their cavern. You froze. What was that about?"

"I don't know what you're talking about."

"What? It may have only been a minute, but it seemed like an eternity before you decided on what you were going to do."

"No, I did not."

" 'Fraid so short stuff." Piers said.

"Yep, I thought I was gonna have to throw you at one of them but felt like I couldn't move myself until you decided." Magh said laughing.

"How dare you think of tossing me as such. And besides, I have so much to choose from so excuse me if I took an extra second to pick the right spell."

"An extra second? It was like you left to evacuate your bowels, but instead just stood there blankly staring at the room." Tymor stated.

"Well, if it is as you say it is, this only furthers my theory that we aren't in control of our own destiny."

"Not again." Magh grunted.

"No, not this." Tymor protested.

"Here we go again." Piers sighed.

"Yes, again. I have told you repeatedly of times when things just didn't seem right. Rooms magically being back in order after we've trashed them. Bartenders, barmaids, and shady characters having very eerily similar faces though claiming they never knew the other person about whom we were talking. So many of the villains we face having very similar voices and accents. And overall, never feeling like were in total control. It's as if there's some unseen force guiding us along and forcing us to do things and making decisions for us. You can't tell me you haven't felt it."

"The last one is easy to explain if you simply put yer faith in your God. Let them guide ye and trust that they have a plan for ye." Tymor explained.

"Ok, oh devout one. What about the villains?"

"Val, of course they all sound alike. They are part of the same cult we've been chasing all this time. They are trying to raise a demon army and we've been trying to stop them for so long." Piers suggested.

"Alright. Then how do you explain all the people looking eerily similar." Val asked.

"Uhm...Val, how long do we stay in these towns and villages? Magh asked.

"A few days. Why?"

"I don't want to sound...uhm...racist? But not every dwarf, no offense."

"None taken." Tymor said.

"Not every human, no offense."

"None taken." Piers shrugged.

"And not every gnome, no offense."

"None taken." Val stated.

"And not all half-orcs, no offense." Turning her head to the left then over to the right in response. "None taken. Are going to stick out when we don't spend much time in one place. All the faces are going to start melding together in our minds. Only those that we interact with more often will be more prominent. We remember those more distinctly and even those will eventually become part of the meld after we've moved on."

"Well, that's...pretty philosophical, especially coming from you. Maybe I have been over thinking this. However, it still doesn't have me convinced. Here are my counter arguments."

Everyone groaned as Val pulled out several scrolls that unrolled many feet. He began to recite his many counter arguments well into the night accompanied by Piers' lyre playing. At some point the others walked off to their bedrolls as Val continued his dissertation not realizing they had all retired for the night. Sorting out the loot would have to wait until another time.

In the morning, the group broke camp and began heading to the village to meet the magistrate to inform him and the locals of the witch's demise. Val must have continued a couple of hours into the evening as his voice sounded quite hoarse and his eyes had darks circles and heavy bags underneath to match. Piers made the most of the situation by continuously pestering Val with songs of conspiracy to mock his theories. Only after Piers noticed Val humming along and ignoring the words due to the repetitive nature of his tune did he stop.

As they rode the four continued their usual banter back and forth recounting their adventures while embellishing their own individual exploits. Even Tymor, who never lied about anything, joined in on the revelry. The stories grew increasingly far-fetched as the hours ticked by. Magh was about to discuss her bout with a cyclops for a third time when Tymor slowed the group as a wagon appeared in the distance. They cautiously approached, not noticing anyone around the wagon.

The dual horse drawn wagon was made of sturdy wood. It was brightly colored in red and accented in orange and yellows. Trinkets and baubles hung from its tresses and swung in the wind. Intricate symbols and designs decorated the walls of the wagon. As the group approached the back of the wagon a short old goblin woman opened the door. She was dressed in a fine woolen red dress and matching conical hat, her hair was graying tied in a long braid down her back. Her pale green skin accented her yellow eyes. She smiled broadly with pointed and broken browning teeth as she saw the four of them at the back door.

"Oh my, welcome travelers! Welcome to Agmara's Accursed Curiosities. How may I help you?"

"Everyone be wary, I'll handle this." Tymor whispered to his team. "Good day madam. We are simply passing through on our way to the village. Do ye have supplies?"

"I have many things. Would you like to have a look?" She turned and opened the door as her smile grew wider.

"Tymor, we should go." Val suggested.

"I agree." Tymor stated. "Madam, on second thought we should be on our way. We want to...by the holy hand of Tyr. Is that an ogre slaying knife?"

Tymor immediately leapt down from his horse and rushed over to the wagon. At the door he stopped, and his eyes grew wide at how large the inside was compared to the actual size of the wagon. He roared with laughter as he went inside and started to look around.

"Please do come in. I'm sure there's something here for all of you." Agmara suggested as she waved her arm for the others to follow.

"I'll handle this he says." Piers mocks as he dismounts his horse and began to head inside.

"No sense in letting the pious one spend all our gold on some holy relic. Let's go." Val agreed.

"Ugh…" Magh groaned.

Once everyone was inside they realized just how large the wagon was. It was not a small wagon, but a full two-story shop. There were weapons and armor racks, shelves with potions, walls of scrolls, tables with trinkets, baubles, and items of various shapes and sizes. Tymor was moving quickly through the shop nearly drooling over the weapons and armor. Then he paused at a table that displayed many items. The one he particularly was looking at was an ivory first with a silver shield affixed to the back of the hand.

"By all things holy, this shop has everything my heart desires and more." Tymor exclaimed.

"Yes, I keep it well stocked. But I must warn you…every item comes at a price." Agmara said.

"Yes, yes. I know how shops work." Tymor stated.

"The price may be more than you expect to pay in the end." Agmara added.

"Yes, I know how regional taxes work as well." He sighed.

"I'm trying to tell you that I'm evil and offering these wares with no regard for the harm they will do!" Agmara said increasingly agitated.

"Argh! Yes, I know goblin alignments and what capitalism is damn it." He responded a little frustrated. "So, how much for the holy symbol?"

"Just take it and get out you moron." She said sounding defeated.

"Ye are too kind madam. I will regale the countryside with tales of yer gratitude and shop of wonders."

"Just…go."

The others stood in shock as Tymor had somehow managed to overcome an enemy before she had a chance to do something bad. As Tymor left the shop the other three nodded in agreement and turned towards Agmara who got a worried look on her face.

"Please don't. You don't understand, I'm cursed to sell these cursed items." She pleaded.

"Aww sweetie. We're simply gonna help remove that curse." Magh stated as she drew her battle axe and charged...

Exiting the wagon last Piers lit an oil lamp and tossed it inside before closing the door. Opening the door again revealed the inside of the small wagon. Wherever the shop was actually located would be burning and appeared that only the goblin knew how to open the door for this portal. The others mounted their horses noticing Tymor was enthralled by his new holy symbol.

"Ready to go Tymor?" Val asked?

"Oh yea, sorry to keep you waiting."

The others laughed as they continued down the road to the village.

A few hours later the party of four arrived at the village. Before receiving any news from the villagers who saw them on the street as they passed, they began to cheer. The four went straight to the magistrate's house to deliver their report and claim their reward. Dismounting and walking into the building the group discovered that the magistrate had extra guards outside. Despite their presence the group was not stopped and allowed entry into the building.

Entering the main foyer, the four of them were met by the magistrate who greeted them and lead them into his study. Offering food and drinks he motioned for everyone to take a seat.

"Seeing you all back here suggests that the witches have been taken care of, is that correct?"

"That is correct. They were easily dispatched." Tymor stated.

"Yes, we had thought so. The wards they had placed upon the village seemed to have lifted the moment they were eliminated."

"Well, we're glad we could help out."

"Oh, you have greatly. In fact, your reward should be taking effect any moment now."

"Taking effect? What do you mean?"

Tymor began to stand as screams were starting to be heard outside the windows. Piers and Magh stood to look out each of them.

"Demons are rising from the ground. They're killing the villagers and other villagers are changing." Piers reported.

"Yep, Same over here." Magh replied. No notion of surprise on her voice.

"It's the damn cult." Val interjected.

"YOU!" Tymor yelled and pointed at the magistrate drawing his sword.

"We should have done this so much sooner. You played right into our plot. The witches were an order of clerics protecting this village from our influence, but no longer."

"I knew it was weird that they didn't put up much of a fight." Magh swore.

"Yes, and now Lord Baphomet will rise and there is nothing you can do. Now, if you'll excuse me." The magistrate turned the stone bust's head of a dragon on his desk and jumped into a hole exposed by a trapdoor.

The doors to the room busted open as two demons covered in barbs entered the room. Tymor wasted no time in engaging the two. Val moved toward the desk as did Piers. Piers worked the dragon bust to open the trap door again as Val prepared a spell.

"Let's go Tymor! They aren't important!" Piers shouted.

"Don't you dare!" Magh shouted looking back at Val who was smiling as he prepared the semantic and verbal components of his spell. Acting quickly, she grabbed Tymor as she took a claw across her back and ran to jump into the hole.

"FIREBALL!" Val shouted.

"YOU ASSHO..." Magh's voice trailed off as she fell into the darkness of the hole after Piers with Tymor in her arms.

The three of them were sliding down a stone chute in complete darkness. All attempts to slow or stop failed as the walls of the chute seemed to be enchanted for this very purpose. As they were sliding uncontrollably an audible blaring began to sound every other second and a blinding light would flash.

"WHAT IS THIS?!" Piers yelled?

"MUST BE SOME SORT OF ALARM!" Tymor replied "THEY'LL KNOW WE'RE COMIN.' BE READY."

The three spilled out a few seconds later into a large dark chamber. A massive cave was rimmed with torches around the base. An altar lay in the center where the magistrate was chanting. The three drew their weapons and prepared to charge as Val launched out of the chute and barreled into them knocking them down.

"OOOWeee that was awesome! I have got to put that in our keep." Val said.

"Can you be serious for even a second?" Tymor grunted.

"What do you mean? I am serious. I need to put one of those in the keep." Val asked puzzled.

"Oh, just shut it and lets go. So, we can stop that blasted noise." Magh complained.

The four charged at the magistrate who remained chanting at the altar as they approached. Magh was the first to reach him and raised her battle axe high as he turned and looked at her.

"You're too late. He's arrived."

The others gathered around the magistrate ready to attack as the cavern began to shake violently. The magistrate then turned his head skyward and looked to the abyssal darkness above them. Tears running down his cheeks and a smile across his face.

"Take me dark lord. I am yours." The magistrate pleaded.

The rumbling grew louder and stronger as the four adventurers turned their head and eyes upward as well. Val instinctively attacked the darkness with a barrage of magic missiles as no one else would be able to attack anything so far away. Despite his attempt a massive pale colored clawed hand appeared in the darkness above. It moved with such speed that no one could react quick enough. It clawed the sides of the cavern and tore through it like paper. It crashed down onto the cavern floor crushing everything to dust and paste.

The hand came crashing down three more times and finally the noise had stopped, and the hand rested still momentarily. Light now flooded the area as the sun was peaking over the horizon. Recoiling back the hand knocked over an empty bottle of Mtn Dew™. It fell onto a crumpled snack bag of Cheetos™ creating a disturbing amount of noise on the wooden floor. The alarm clock balanced on the edge of the nightstand hanging on by its cord plugged into the wall now that the hand lifted off of it.

Sitting up in bed Willow rubbed her eyes and yawned. Grinning she reached over and opened the drawer on the nightstand. Pulling out a notebook and pen she began writing with vigor.

"That was a crazy dream, but a great campaign idea. If my group wants to be a bunch of murder hobos, then they've got another thing comin'."

The dungeon mistress giggled as she wrote out the next campaign. She planned on using the characters she dreamed up in the overall scenario to keep them living on longer. She could not wait until their next gaming session of Dungeons and Dragons™.

I:X:XII

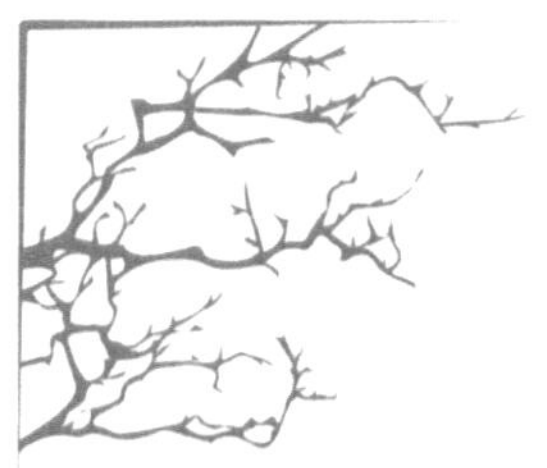

A Message

It was a hot and sunny summer day. The beginning of festival season had officially kicked off and with that came renaissance fairs, 4-H festivals, music festivals, art festivals, pop-up carnivals, street fairs, and many more events than Miguel could even think of attending. He had his food truck setup, and his employees were fast at work turning orders. In preparation for today's food truck competition, he made sure he was well prepared and well stocked.

The menu was limited due to the competition, but he made sure to have a couple favorites on it for return customers. The biggest issue during the competition was how long people had to wait in line, so he limited the items that took longer and with that the price was also higher so not many ordered the items. Other categories included taste, price, portion size, uniqueness, and overall satisfaction. Miguel knew he could not win every category but strived to place in at least two.

He watched from the side of his truck as people ordered his food and were surprised at how quickly they received it. They also genuinely enjoyed the food from the look of it as they sat and ate, not that he was surprised, he was just happy to see the expressions on everyone's faces as they enjoyed their meal. Cards were passed out with every meal with a QR code to scan or link to go to in order to vote so they could easily complete the process. He was pleased to see most were doing it way before they had finished any of his meals.

The back door of the truck swung open causing him to jump by the sudden noise behind him. He looked over to see that his sample cart was ready to go. With the help of his employee, they lowered it to the ground.

"I'll be back in about an hour. Call me if you need anything."

"Okay jefe."

Miguel carted his samples over to the food truck tent for all the other food truck owners to try out his food. He would also try the other trucks food as well and vote. The only rule was that you could not vote for your own truck. Wheeling into the tent he moved over to his designated spot and set up the food along with his menu and nutritional information and watched as everyone else began to set up their stations as well.

Here in the tent the truck owners discussed assorted topics about their trucks from storage space to generator size. Some brought their families along and others had employees stand in for them if they were too busy. Occasionally, a truck would just drop off food simply because they had no personnel available. Regardless, this was the best way to be able to taste all the great food without having to stand in the lines and wait.

Miguel engaged with friends he had made over the years from attending many venues. Catching up they grabbed a plate and made their way around the tent and grabbed a little something from most vendors. He did not care for the vegan options personally, but still grabbed what looked appetizing. After gathering their food, they sat at a table and began to eat.

It was difficult to get caught up on things when everyone was eating such delicious food. They only paused what they were saying or interrupted each other to state how good something was or how it needed to be tried right that second. The tent was alive with conversations and laughter while everyone engaged with one another. However, that changed quickly when Miguel started to get hot.

"Hey Miguel, you alright?" Rob, a driver of an Italian food truck asked.

"Yea, it's just getting hot." He replied.

"Are you sure? You're getting pretty red. Was it something spicy?"

"You know...*cough*...I can eat the spiciest stuff here." Miguel tried to take a drink and found he could not swallow it.

"Then I think you're having an allergic reaction. Are you allergic to anything?"

"*COUGH* Peanuts...*cough*" he pushed away from the table and doubled over vomiting on the grass floor.

"DID ANYONE COOK WITH PEANUTS?" Rob shouted as he stood and rushed over to Miguel as he fell to the ground. Looking around no one that Miguel had eaten from had their arm raised or responded.

"Had to be one of the vendors not here. Damn it. Stay with me buddy." Rob slapped his cheeks trying to keep Miguel conscious. Many people were calling 911 and a couple ran to get help from the EMT tent.

"Eh...*cough*...pen n...*cough*...ruck" Miguel struggled to get out information to Rob where his Epi-pen was located.

"Pen? Ruck?" Rob stared at Miguel trying to piece together what he was trying to say when it came to him. "He's got an Epi-pen in his truck! Someone go get it. It'll be quicker than everyone else. We got you buddy just stay with us." Rob kept patting his cheeks. At least Miguel thought he did. His face had gone numb, and he could no longer see due to his eyes swelling shut.

The light filtering in through swollen eyes was dimming rapidly as his breath became more and more difficult. The last thing he heard was something about stabbing him in the leg before everything went black.

Standing in his truck Miguel took orders and passed them along to his cooks. A man in sunglasses and a backpack wearing a leather jacket approached to order. It was a little warm for a jacket, but he must have ridden a motorcycle. He was friendly and ordered a dorilotes walking taco and water. Taking his money and giving him his change. The man left a great tip and went on his way. Miguel thought he recognized the man but was not certain who he reminded him of that he knew.

Continuing to take orders he served a little girl in a princess outfit and her mother, a group of teenagers that barely looked up from their phones, and an elderly couple before deciding to taking a break. Stepping out of the back of the truck and into the heat of the day was actually a drop in temperature from the inside of his food truck. He had an instant feeling of coolness from the wind hitting his sweat soaked shirt as he stepped out into the lesser of the two heated environments. Walking over to the picnic tables behind the food trucks he sat down and drank his water.

He listened to the live music in the background despite not being able to hear it very well over the roar of his truck's generator. He mainly bobbed his head to the bass that broke through the sound. Even with the roar of the generator the air was filled with sounds of laughter, bells and whistles of games and incoherent microphones discussing various announcements or narrating a nearby show. Muffled by the generator most of the sounds and what came through was mainly a distortion of inaudible nonsense, so he decided to get to a better position. He got up to stand at the front of the truck as the sounds became clearer and watched the crowd as the ensemble of joy filled his ears that made his work all worthwhile.

A loud popping sound began to ring out across the area. Miguel looked around to see who was setting off fireworks when the sounds of joy turned into a cacophony of chaos. Screams and shouting began to erupt from everywhere. His first thought was that the group of teenagers may have been responsible for the popping.

He could not have been more wrong. Half of them lay on the ground several yards in front of him as the others were hobbling off screaming and covered in blood. The mother and daughter lay nearby still holding hands as they laid motionless. The elderly man kneeled over his wife's body, an emotionless expression of disbelief on his face.

The door to his food truck forcefully swung open at the back as his employees ran to flee the area. More popping sounds rang out and it was at this point that Miguel realized they were shots as the bullets ripped through the back of his truck and the bodies of his employees. He quickly took cover behind the front of the truck.

Frightened to move, he remained where he was until he felt confident he could escape to safety. Before deciding to move, more shots rang out much closer to the back of his truck. The bullets ricocheted off the nearby pavement, visibly taking chunks out of the asphalt.

The shots seemed to be coming from the area in front of the trucks, so he decided to move along the back of the trucks to avoid being seen. Miguel crawled to the backside of his truck along the front bumper and peeked his head around the corner. He froze in terror as his eyes were met with the barrel of a gun only inches from his face. He could only see the barrel of the gun and a silhouette of a man behind it wearing a leather jacket as his vision went black with a flash of light.

Miguel gasped awake. He could not see very well but was able to breath even though it being difficult. A hand firmly yet delicately laid on his chest as he attempted to get up.

"Mr. Gutierrez, please calm down. You're in an ambulance on the way to the hospital. Don't try to talk you have a breathing tube in as your throat is still swollen shut. We're going to give you something that will put you back to sleep now that we know you're fine, so you don't further injure yourself. Is that ok?"

While he could not talk he attempted to move his head up and down. To signify his agreement. The next thing he knew he was waking up in a hospital bed with an IV in his arm with his family in the room. No longer groggy he suddenly remembered what had happened.

"Did they get the shooter? How many people died? Is Carlos, Juan, and Sonia alright? How bad are their injuries?" He asked with urgency and concern.

"Sweetheart, there was no shooter." His wife said just as concerned.

"Yes, there was. I was taking orders and took a break, and he began shooting. I think it was the man in the leather jacket. Where is the police? I can describe him."

"Honey, that was a dream. You weren't taking orders. Someone had cooked their food in peanut oil and not listed it on their nutritional card. That's why you had a reaction."

"A dream? You're kidding. It was so real."

"Yes. A dream. Rob saved you by getting someone to your Epi-Pen in the truck. A minute longer and you may not have made it. The vendor had his license revoked almost immediately. Evidently more than just you had an incident before they were found out and shut down. Though yours was the most severe."

"How long have I been out?"

"It's been almost three days."

"Oh no, what about the contest?"

"That is what you're worried about?"

"Well, you told me there was no shooter and it was just a dream. That I'm doing fine now obviously. What else is there?"

"We won in taste, time of preparation, portion size, and overall satisfaction. I guess we got the sympathy vote."

"I wouldn't say that. We worked hard for that. Though I didn't expect to win all that."

"Yea, well you'll have plenty of time to gloat, sympathy vote or not, the season is still fresh. You're expected to release tomorrow. I'll be back then to pick you up. Love you."

"Love you too."

Miguel kissed his wife and hugged his kids before they left. He sat up for a long time after and even into the night thinking about the dream. He couldn't be making it up as it felt so real. The people, the place, the sounds, the man. It scared him to death. If it had not happened yet he was going to make sure he would stop it before it happened.

He went to the police officers with a description of the man to file a report. However, without evidence there was nothing they could do as these events already had security and adding additional assets on dreams and hunches would not persuade them. The security at the festivals began to laugh at Miguel and calling him paranoid. Even new venues were aware of his warnings before he arrived to tell them to be on the lookout for such a person.

Weeks and months went by, and Miguel lived in fear in his truck taking orders expecting the man to arrive one day. He spent extra money to reinforce his truck shutters and doors in case he needed to barricade his employees, himself, and anyone else inside. He bought a pistol and took classes to learn how to shoot and also got a concealed carry permit. He had also bought a shotgun for his truck as well and kept it in a locked box under the cabinets to not freak out his employees. He wanted to ensure he was prepared for the day should it ever arrive.

Years had passed and Miguel had still remembered the dream vividly. If only he had seen something at that particular festival that would remind him of what the day would be, or where the event would be located. He hated himself for not seeing those details. Lost in thought about the dream he took orders as usual. The security guards no longer made fun of him daily and had all but forgotten about crazy Miguel's story. However, he would be reminded every-so-often that at least someone remembered when they would approach his truck wearing a leather jacket. They had burst out in laughter when his eyes would go wide.

"Welcome, what can I get for you sir?"

"Hey amigo, I'll have a dorilotes please. Oh, and a water." The man requested.

"No problem sir. You can check your total pay on the tablet if everything is correct."

"Yea looks great. You have a good day."

"You too sir, you can pick up your food at the next window."

Preoccupied with his thoughts Miguel barely glanced at the man while taking the order. His phone vibrated signifying there was a tip added to the order which he would look at later to tally up for the day and split among everyone. The next customer approached, and he went to take the order again barely paying attention.

"Welcome, what can I get for you?"

"I'm sorry can you give us a second? What would you like to eat sweetie?" Hiding his sigh Miguel put his receipt book and pen down on the counter and looked up at the lady ordering and prompted him to put on a warm smile as he waited. However, instead his eyes widened, and jaw dropped as the woman was addressing her daughter who was dressed in a princess outfit. He looked behind them to see the elderly couple waiting patiently behind the group of zombie teens flipping through their phones.

"It's today." He muttered.

"What's that jefe?" Carlos asked.

"The shooting Carlos, it's today."

"Oh jefe. Not this again bro."

"Just shut up Carlos." Miguel quietly told him and turned toward the lady and her daughter. "I'm sorry ma'am, we've just been alerted of an emergency in the park. If you would like to come inside and take shelter we are about to lock up. That goes for you as well kids and you two also. Just come to the back of the truck."

Miguel closed down the shutters and shut off the grills. He reached under the cabinets, pulled out the shotgun case, and unlocked it and handed it to Carlos. He then drew his pistol and chambered a round making sure it was ready to go and re-holstered it to conceal it again. As he finished prepping the truck a knock came at the door. He opened it to see the mother and daughter and the old couple. The teens were nowhere to be seen.

"I don't think they heard you. They just saw you shut down and walked off."

"That's all right. I'll find them." Miguel let the four people in, though it was cramped in the tiny space. "Carlos keep them safe and keep this door locked. No one gets in. I'll keep the generator running so you can keep the fans on, let them eat and drink whatever they'd like on the house."

"Ma'am did you see what way the man in the leather jacket went?"

"Uhm, sorry no. I was busy with my little girl trying to decide what to eat."

"I did, son." Said the old man. "Thought it was odd to be wearing that jacket in this heat. Watched him walk off towards the pavilion."

"Thanks, I'll start there."

Miguel left the truck and heard the door lock behind him as he walked off in the direction of the pavilion. The grounds were littered with people in this area getting food from the vendors. Port-a-potties were lined up near the pavilion and he decided to stand and look for the man there. Gazing out of the crowded pavilion and eating patrons the man in the leather jacket was nowhere to be seen.

He looked frantically as he knew his time was running short. Back and forth he glanced and still he did not spot the man. Frustrated, he was about to move on when he got a tap on his shoulder.

"Hey friend, that dorilotes was amazing." The man in the leather jacket said graciously. "Are you in line for the johns?"

"Oh, gracias amigo. Si, I'm in line, but go ahead."

"No that's alright partner. Be my guest you were here first."

"No, it's alright I need to go numero dos."

"Ah, say no more. Much appreciated. I'll be feeling that myself after that delicious food. Just a matter of time I guarantee." Laughing the man rubbed his gut. "Say, you aren't afraid of fireworks are ya?

"Me? No, why?"

"Well, that's good, cause there's gonna be some going off in about five minutes. Don't want that deuce to come outta ya prematurely." He said with a menacing smile winking at Miguel.

"Oh, I'll be fine. Oh, look that one just opened up for you." Miguel pointed as the man thanked him and moved over to the port-a-potty.

Miguel waited anxiously outside the toilets for him to emerge drawing his gun out of it's holster and tucking it into his crossed arms so he could stop him before he started killing people. Watching the doors, he saw the backpack strap fall out of the bottom of the door as he took it off inside. A couple other stalls seemed to have straps hanging out as people had placed their bags on the floor to make room to use the facilities. The straps in his door began to move as the man was getting ready to come out. Miguel readied himself as the door swung open.

The door swung open, and the man exited the bathroom with a plague doctor mask on and large red package in his hand. He walked back over to Miguel putting his backpack back on while trying not to drop the package.

"I told you there's gonna be fireworks. This a 5000-cap roll. My friends are all over the park ready to light theirs in...two minutes. Better get in there before all hell breaks loose." Laughing he walked off to where he was planning on setting his roll off around the park. Miguel reholstered his pistol doing his best to not be seen.

Miguel was sure he was right. How could he be so wrong? Everyone was there from his dream. All the pieces fit. Why did it play out like this? To not appear to be creeping on someone in the toilets he decided to enter the port-a-potty the guy had used. Reaching for the door, the stall next to his unlocked and the door began to swing open as he was entering. As Miguel turned to shut to door due to a broken spring he saw the person leaving the stall next to his exiting with a rifle in his hands. Immediately he drew his pistol and aimed at the man who was also wearing a black leather jacket.

"DROP IT NOW!" Miguel commanded as loud as he could causing people to take cover nearby, shouting 'gun', and start running from the area.

Turning slowly the man faced Miguel. He had a mask on, but Miguel could see from his eyes that he was shocked. The man slowly lifted a hand up to his head and removed his mask. It was Rob. He was the vendor that lost his license due to negligent use of peanut oil and not properly including it on his labels.

"How did you know?"

"I didn't Rob. I didn't even know it was you that lost your license since you said you were planning on working down south for a while. It was almost a year before I found out. I don't blame you for that."

"I didn't ask you for your sympathy. These people ruined my life. You ruined my life. It's people like you that make this business difficult in the first place. Forcing us to change good recipes because of your weak immune systems. Causing us to use more expensive and exotic cooking materials because your weak stomachs can't handle this or that. Demanding that we have a vegan option, a gluten free option. Complain, complain, complain. So, they're all gonna pay Miguel."

"You don't have to do this Rob. You can still walk away from this no harm done."

"No Miguel, I can't." He began to raise the rifle towards Miguel but had no chance of shooting him first as Miguel was still aiming at him. As soon as Rob began moving Miguel conducted a Mozambique firing drill on him that he had learned in his firearms training putting two rounds through Rob's chest and a third into his head.

Rob dropped lifeless after the fatal shots and as if a fanfare were playing the fireworks began to pop off all around the park. This time the popping sound would not result in people losing their lives. That little girl would be with her mother, the old couple would still be together, and the group of teens would flock together and text each other memes a foot apart from one another.

Miguel removed his magazine, emptied his pistol, and laid it on the ground. He also removed the rifle from Rob as well as two other pistols he had on him. He moved them off to the side in case he was not dead and wanted to react by grabbing a weapon if he happened to come back like some cliche horror film.

Regardless of seeing multiple people on their phones Miguel called the police and told them what happened. He did not mention how he knew this time but was sure it would come up in his past reports. Unsure if the dream was a vision of the future, a form of Déjà Vu, or some sort of time travel, one thing he did know was that he stopped it from happening. That is the way he saw it and that was all that mattered to Miguel.

11-B:I:J

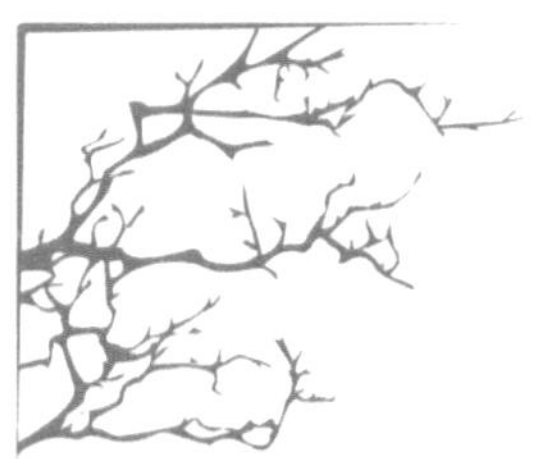

Transmigration

"Margaret Elizabeth Bishop having been found guilty of heresy, promiscuity, making a pact with Satan, and witchcraft. The latter of which has caused Henry Caldwell's cow to dry up, David Smith's chickens to run off, young Frederick Dunmore to become impotent, and worst of all have caused the Thorp's youngest daughter Susan to disappear." Jacob Saddlemire, the regions witch hunter, pointed as he accused her of the crimes in front of the villagers gathered around the pyre.

"I have done none of those things sir." Margaret pleaded.

The smell of oil-soaked wood filled her nostrils as the wind on the night air blew through her sweat soaked hair. She was bound to a single post in the middle of a pile of wood stacked several feet tall. The rope bound her arms to her sides and her back to the post from her knees to her shoulders.

"Lies and slander." He mocked. "She still denies it despite the evidence against her. Her livestock thrives and yet Mr. Smith and Mr. Caldwell now suffer due to her witchcraft."

"No."

"Yes. And Mr. Dunmore can no longer lie with a woman after lying with you."

"That's not true. I have never lain with him. It is not my fault he prefers the company of men over women."

"How dare you make these false accusations." Frederick yelled.

"False? I'm sure William LaMonte would say...OW!" she screamed as someone threw a rock at her.

"You see how she continues to spin a web of lies to turn us against each other? This is how she casts her vile sorcery. Do not listen to her lies." Jacob continued.

"These are not lies. I have nothing to..."

"SILENCE!" he shouted while throwing a hand into the air. "You will speak no longer unless given the opportunity. I will ask thee one last time. Where is the Thorp's daughter?"

"I do not know."

"You were the last person seen with her when you refused to give her an apple from your basket."

"The apples were for everyone after our sermon on Sunday. She was being selfish and wanted one before and I denied her. Everyone saw me there. How could I have done something?"

"You see, she admits it."

"Wait, no"

"You deny being with her before service?"

"No, but..."

"Then, where is she? It was only after the service that anyone realized she was gone as she was not with her friends nor her parents. The incident you described happened a good quarter hour before service began. So, where is she?"

"I know not of her whereabouts. She went into the woods upset she had not gotten an apple. As I have stated many times."

"Into the woods you say? And in the direction of your farm? We have heard enough. Your vile tongue cannot help but spew the truth behind your twisted lies. Bring forth the torches." He raised his arms signaling a few men to step forward. He also stepped closer to Margaret and snatched a torch from one of the men as well as he approached the unlit pyre.

"Behold, a woman who paid with her soul for Satan's unholy knowledge! Let her sinful presence be purged from us as her sins fuel this holy flame!" Staring directly at Margaret he tossed his torch at her feet onto the oil-soaked wood, igniting it with ease. The other men tossed on their torches as well setting the pyre ablaze from all sides.

"Nooo..." Margaret screamed as the flames began to rise around her...

Brandt loved his life as an influencer. If he was not making videos, he was editing videos, producing innovative ideas, or posting his latest adventures on all his different platforms. With over a million followers he had an image to uphold and the only way to do that was to constantly create content. He was known for being reckless with his parkour stunts and pranks as well as always doing the most random and absurd dares spurred on by his friends.

He was editing his latest escapade where he released a dozen squirrels loose in a hunting and fishing store. He did well to capture all the chaos that was caused by the squirrels but made sure to edit out the part where he was fined. He had also got his friend fired from the store who let them in through the back entrance. Not feeling any remorse, he laughed as he edited the footage showing no regret for his actions. Once completed he began uploading it to his platforms.

"Dudes, it's already got over a thousand views and it's only been a minute." Brandt told his two friends playing video games in the room with him.

"Awesome man." Derrick replied not looking away from the game.

"Yea...cool." Kevin grumbled.

"Oh, c'mon Kev. We'll find you another job. Besides what's better than hangin' out all day?"

"Yea, you're right. My boss sucked anyhow."

"That's the spirit. Hey let's head downtown. I hear there's a protest or something happening that we can check out."

"Heck yea. I dare you to get a cop to beat you up." Derrick suggested as he put down the controller and got up from the couch.

"Pfft. Challenge accepted sucker." Brandt replied.

"Then let's go."

The three of them loaded up into Brandt's car and drove downtown and parked in a garage. Walking to where the protest was located the streets were lightly populated by people heading to various appointments and businesses throughout the area. When the young men arrived to the square where the protest was scheduled to be they found it was void of anyone carrying a sign or any type of protesting occurring at all.

"Oh man, this sucks." Brandt whined.

"Well, what do we do now?" Derrick asked.

"Could do some parkour videos on the rails, stairs, and bollards." Kevin suggested.

"Nah, we've got plenty of that. We need something fresh."

"We haven't done a disgusting food video in a while. I bet you won't snort some wasabi with your sushi." Derrick proposed with a grin.

"You know, as much as that sounds like a good challenge...pass. Another time. Still looking for something else...THERE!"

Brandt pointed across the street to a corner. Positioned there was a man with a sign that read "JESUS LOVES YOU." He also had a bookstand that had an assortment of bibles and other religious texts on display. He was an older gentleman conservatively dressed in slacks and a dress shirt with a sweater vest over top of it. Brandt pulled out his phone and selfie stick and began to record.

"Good afternoon my peeps. I'm downtown with Derrick and Kev, say hey guys."

"Hey."

"Yo."

"Anyways, we're live here on this lovely day and planned on being in a protest, but it must have been broken up early. But, have no fear I have a treat for you. We are going to go talk with a man about Jesus. I know, I know. But Brandt aren't you an Atheist?" he said, rolling his eyes. "Yes, and that's why this is going to be so much fun. Let's go."

Crossing the street Brandt laughed and breathed rhythmically as he was pumping himself up for his interview. Kevin and Derrick were pumping him up as they walked and all three were nearly hit by a car while not paying attention to the traffic.

"Hey watch it." Brandt yelled as he made it to the corner flipping the car off with his free hand.

"That was a close one, son." The man stated. "Seems you got an angel looking out for you boys."

"I highly doubt that old timer." Brandt snapped.

"Oh? Why is that?"

"Because I'm an Atheist. So, there aren't angels watching over me and "He" sure as hell doesn't love me." He said pointing at the man's sign.

"Jesus loves everyone. He gave his life for us all. Believers and non-believers alike."

"That's a bunch of crap. Why would he do something so dumb when so many don't believe in it?"

"Because you are free to believe in what you want. He knows you will find your way, one way or another."

"Wow, that's amazing. And I bet it's all in that book huh?"

"Yes, it is."

"And what will you do if I steal it?"

"Well stealing is wrong but be my guest as they are free."

Brandt was growing frustrated with the conversation. Even more so that the old man was not showing any sort of anger towards his insults. He smiled at the man as he stepped toward the bookstand and reached forward to act as if he was going to grab a book. Instead, he knocked over the stand while he continued to livestream the event.

"Dude, why'd you do that?" Kevin shouted.

"Because I'm offended by the display. You don't see me out here trying to convert more Atheists. Not that I need to, this stuff is ridiculous."

Stepping a couple feet away from the toppled stand and books Brandt scoffed as Kevin started helping the man pick up the books. Derrick joined Brandt cheering him on to his followers that were logged in and watching his stream.

"Yea, that's right. If your religion was the true religion you wouldn't need to be out here on the street bothering innocent people with your propaganda. This is offensive to not only me but should be to all of you that follow his religion. This is simply embarrassing. You would never catch me...Ooof."

So enthralled in his streaming Brandt did not see the two large men crossing the street. Standing in the middle of the sidewalk the men walked through them bumping both Brandt and Derrick to the side without a word and kept walking.

"What the hell bro? Maybe say excuse me next time?" Brandt shouted.

Both of the large men stopped and turned around. One of them walked backed towards Brandt as Derrick retreated to the bookstand.

"I'm not your bro, bitch."

"That's not what I meant." Trying to back pedal his words.

"Then what did you mean bitch?"

"I just meant it...I just meant I was sorry for not getting out of your way sir."

"Yea, that's what I thought." Pausing the man looked at Brandt's phone that he lowered. "You recording right now?"

"Uhm...live streaming. Shit."

"Oh, damn, so all your followers got to see you look like a bitch huh. I tell you what, I'll help you redeem that. Pull your phone back up and greet your fan base."

"Hey everyone. So, yea that was a little scary, but I'm ok." Brandt said with a shaky voice but regaining his confidence.

"Alright, now tell them bye but keep it on for a few more seconds."

"Ok everyone. Hope you enjoyed the stream I'll see you next time when we're at the skate park pulling off some sick tricks."

"Yea, no you won't."

Brandt's face went from his normal cocky and confident look to confused to terrified in seconds as he dropped his selfie stick and phone. The man came at him and stabbed him repeatedly in the chest. He could not tell how many times he had been stabbed as each new wound erased the pain of the previous. He began to choke up blood as he started to crumple forward into the man. After a few more stabs the man let Brandt fall to the ground as he ran off with his friend.

"Kevin let's get out of here before they come back." Is all Brandt heard Derrick shout as he lied on the ground beginning to bleed out...

Jacquie laid in her hospital bed in a weakened state. The beeping of the heart monitors echoed through the hollow white room. Multiple IVs dripped into her through tubes in her hands and arms. She could barely turn her knit cap covered bald head to look at her parents at her bedside let alone keep her eyes open. Under her hospital blanket her body had shriveled up to a skeleton of her former self and she relied more on tubes and devices to maintain her bodily functions than on her own capacity.

The leukemia had been beaten when she was younger, but the doctors missed some of it and after a couple of years of it going unchecked it grew rapidly and unexpectedly. Barely fourteen years old, she knew she did not have a full life, but she lived it as fully as she could with the time she had. Even now as she lay in bed, she relished this moment with her parents as they read to her from her Harry Potter™ books.

Unable to move she listened as they read the story to her. Her mother stuttered and started to sob, and her father picked up the reading as he put his arm around her. Her father's voice always soothed her, and she found herself getting sleepy. However, the pain she was constantly in prevented her from sleeping without medication. Knowing she was not going to be around much longer she wanted to be with her parents as long as she could, so she resisted taking her medication as much as possible.

Coughing, her mom stopped sobbing and rushed to her side to wipe her mouth and give her a drink of water. She loved her mom immensely and her only regret was the heartbreak she knew her parents were going through and would be going through when she was gone.

"I...I'm...sorry mama." Jacquie squeaked.

"Oh honey. You have nothing to be sorry for."

"But mama, you're so sad."

"Yes baby, but we know you're going to a much better place free of all this pain."

"But I don't want to leave you alone."

"Sweetheart, we'll be together again. You don't need to worry about that."

Jacquie and her mom began to cry together as her mom hugged her. She was only slightly comforted by her mom's words. The hug provided more comfort for her as it was something she could feel and hold onto to. The words began to sound empty the more she thought about them. She still believed in God and prayed that she would be with him in the end, but the pain and suffering she was enduring tore at her faith.

She continued to lie in her mother's arms with her eyes shut when her body erupted in pain. Her morphine button had fallen out of her hand as she tried to press it. She screamed as her body convulsed under the pain. Her mother grabbed the button and pressed it for her until Jacquie calmed down.

"Thank you, mama."

"You're welcome baby."

"I love you mama."

"I love you too, Jacquie."

Jacquie closed her eyes as the morphine took hold. The pain faded away as did the beeping of the heart monitor that became a solid continuous tone that diminished into silence...

Margaret wailed as the flames began to blister her flesh. Her feet were in excruciating pain as the flames closed in on her. It was becoming difficult to breathe, but the pain allowed her to keep wailing. Through the rising fire she could see the villagers watching on in horrific fascination as she burned. Among the onlookers Margaret witnessed a sight that turned her pain into rage. A dirty weary-looking girl in a tattered dress was walking towards the crowd. A girl Margaret knew as Susan Thorp was being hugged and greeted by her family.

"I told you I was not responsible." Margaret wailed. "This girl looks as though she was lost. I worship no devil or demon. I have not sold my soul. I serve the Earth Mother and have blessed this village with her gifts. You all have squandered them. I curse you all. I plead the Earth Mother to curse you all for your sins."

Margaret smiled as she succumbed to the flames. The heat charred her flesh as she felt herself blister and boil as life faded from her. The light and heat of the flames extinguished in an instant and she found herself in a dark garden in front of a massive tree illuminated by moonlight.

"Welcome sister." A friendly voice called out to her.

"Where am I?" Margaret asked, looking around the gardens. Glowing orbs of assorted colors floated throughout the area and into the darkness beyond.

"You are here in the ethereal. You have been here before, but only once. The more you return the more you'll remember."

"Then I am to meant to return to the realm of the Earth Mother?"

"Yes. You will return to my realm."

"Forgive my ignorance, Earth Mother." She pleaded as she prostrated herself before her.

"Please rise sister. Here we are equals. We all share in the knowledge and gifts of the Tree of Life. The wisps around you are friends and foes alike that sought to exploit that knowledge and are paying the price. The more severe the exploitation the further they are cast from the Tree."

"Could I talk with them?"

"Yes, but you would be wise to heed that warning. It is why when you return it is not always the way you expect. You do not remain here long before being reborn."

"I understand." Margaret began walking around the garden, taking in the massiveness of the Tree of Life. Its branches extended high into the night sky and the trunk was wider than she could see around. It was as if the Tree itself was a massive wall blocking entry to the opposite side of it. The bark looked rough and ageless but was smooth to the touch and left no marring on her hand after she brushed against it. She was in awe of its immense size and power. As she released her hand she began to emit a glowing light from within chest. She turned toward the Earth Mother with wide eyes.

"It is time sister. You a returning. Embrace your new life. I will see you again. Blessed be."

The light erupted from her as she was consumed by it. She tumbled through the light formless as the light took on a tunneled shape. She was hurled through the tunnel at great speed that came to sudden halt. The blinding light ended in darkness, and she found she could not open her eyes. Her arms and legs shifted, but they lacked strength. A sudden push from behind startled her; unable to see who or what had done it. Another push ensued, followed by another. Unable to endure any further, she finally let out a scream.

"MEOW!"

She froze wondering why she made that sound. Then became berated by something licking her furiously. Unable to do anything she succumbed to the treatment and realized it was calming her and she began purring. It had finally dawned upon her that she was reborn as a cat and was reinforced when she heard a voice.

"Felicia, you delivered a black one. The Earth Mother has blessed me. I shall call you Maggie. My new familiar has arrived. You have done such a wonderful job Felicia."

Margaret thought about what the Earth Mother had mentioned, and this must have been what she meant when not every return is what is expected. She knew she had much to learn, and she looked forward to experiencing it all.

1:2:4:5:7:9-D:E:F:G:H

The old man knelt at Brandt's side trying to apply pressure to his many wounds. A crowd began to gather as word spread of the incident. Many phones were out as Brandt lay bleeding, but none were on the line with emergency services. All were facing Brandt recording or live streaming him. His own phone attached to the selfie stick was lying a few feet from him still live streaming. The angle showed his head and the old man kneeling over him to his followers.

"Lie still son. Help will be here soon." The old man assured him. "Is there anyone you want me to call?"

Brandt tried to speak but coughed up blood. So, he shook his head no. His breathing became difficult and raspy as his chest was becoming tight. All Brandt could think about was how his friends had abandoned him and left him alone. How no one defended him or ran to his side except the man he insulted. How all these people stood around filming him instead of helping him.

"Son, would you like me to pray for you?"

Brandt was shocked to hear the request. Despite the man offering it as a kind gesture Brandt still refused it by shaking his head no. The man simply shrugged and closed his eyes and bowed his head regardless while maintaining pressure on his wounds. Brandts own eyes were difficult to keep open as his breath was getting even more shallow. The raggedness was increasing as well as the pain in his chest.

Sirens began to fill the air when the pain started to become unbearable. He took a few gasps of empty air as he fell into emptiness.

Brandt found himself in darkness cramped and unable to move for a long time. Eventually he was able to free his upper body and start crawling upward out of a dark sludge. He could not help but feel he was digging out of a coffin. He struggled upward and soon was able to spread his legs out below him to assist his movement upward.

Struggling for what felt like days Brandt finally emerged from the sludge. The sun shone upon him, and he was able to spread his arms. They felt weak from the climb and provided minimal assistance in climbing out of the sludge. It felt great feeling the sun upon his flesh. He could not open his eyes. Feeling that the sludge was still all over him slowly falling off he would not force them open and risk getting any inside his eyes. The sounds of nature flooded his senses, and he was unaware of where he was located. A strong wind blew through the area and Brandt bent backwards at the force of it. His arms flailed as it whipped over him powerless to stand up against it.

The realization of being reincarnated as a sapling hit Brandt hard. He was unsure if he would grow into a fully developed tree that lived centuries or be trampled by wildlife or campers before his stem ever hardened. His memories were fading fast, and he had already forgotten who he had used to be except for his name and a few of his friends and events. He remembered what had happened to him and could feel marks along his stem where he had been stabbed and wondered if they would still show when his bark hardened. Only time would tell if Brandt would be given the opportunity to grow or wilt.

2:6:9-1:II:IV:V:VI:XIII

I n the silence Jacquie found herself able to sit up in her bed with no difficulty. The quiet was replaced with a beautiful melodious sound that came from every direction as the ceiling opened up illuminating the dimly lit room into a brilliant radiance of white light. A corridor of light leading to a distant point beckoned her with warmth.

Looking into the room as she began to lift upward out her bed she saw mother crying into her limp hand. Her father standing solemnly behind her mother embracing her in his arms trying to provide comfort and remain strong for them both. Her doctor and nurses flooded into the room to react to the monitors. None were able to do anything but tried providing some sort of condolences as she had agreed to signing a do not resuscitate due to the terminal status of her condition.

In her current state of no more pain and suffering she finally grasped what her mother was saying. The warmth of the light and the soothing sound of music promised her of new life. She let herself lift into the light as she floated higher. In seconds she was at the ceiling of her room, moments later at the roof of the hospital, then seemingly high in air. The ray of light looked as though it were a beam of sunshine breaking through the clouds. Even higher she ascended faster and faster through endless clouds until she stood face to face with a being of pure light.

"My child, you have come to me too soon. My plan for you has not been fulfilled. Worry not of the troubles of your past. They will bother you no longer in the life ahead of you. Be at peace, return to the Earth, and live again."

The being raised its arm and Jacquie's body became the form of a ball of light and began to descend back down the vortex of light. Travelling back down she was excited to be with her family again. Oh, to see her parents as she would wake up on the table. Would she be healed of the disease? His words were short but so comforting.

Passing through the clouds Jacquie had forgotten why she was excited. She was also confused as to why she called herself Jacquie. Was that her name? Despite her confusion she embraced the excitement and enjoyed the travel through this tunnel of light. Soon a figure of a woman came into sight as she entered a large building. She slowed and stopped in front of the woman who seemed frightened and shocked to see her, a ball of light, floating in the light.

The woman reached forward and as Jacquie the orb moved towards her curiously. She wrapped around the woman's hand and knew in an instant that she was her earthly mother. She exhumed feelings of love and happiness as the woman's eyes widened and her fear disappeared as she gave the warmest smile. Jacquie moved away from her hand even though she wanted to continue to wrap the woman in her warmth and moved down into the room below where human chaos ensued. Her earthly mother's body was on a table surrounded by nurses and the doctor while two nurses were around the body of the baby she was meant to occupy. Not hesitating another moment, she moved to the body and melded with it.

The doctor emerged from the delivery room and told the orderlies to leave. He looked exhausted and had to physically collect himself to stand up straight and address Robert.

"Robert, you have my deepest sympathies. We were unable to stop the bleeding in Anna. We did all we could to save her."

"You bastard! You could have at least let me stay in there to be with them. Now I have no one and I couldn't even be with them when they passed."

"Mr. Hutchins, you misunderstand. Your daughter survived. The nurse will be out as soon as she's ready to go to the nursery."

"What?"

"Yes, you probably would have heard her, but she didn't cry. She simply opened her eyes and started looking around as if she could understand what was happening, but she's sleeping now."

The doors of the room opened, and a couple nurses came out pushing a cart with the baby wrapped up. Eyes closed with a smile on her little face.

"Mr. Hutchins, we don't usually allow anyone to escort the baby to the nursery after delivery, but given the circumstances would you like to come with us?"

Shaking his head yes, Robert fought back tears as he saw his child on the cart.

"Mr. Hutchins, we will take care of alerting the next of kin while you get settled. We've already prepared a room for you." The doctor instructed.

"Please follow us sir." The nurses led the way and tried their best to calm Robert's nerves. "What is your little girl's name going to be?

"Anna wanted to name her after her grandmother, Jaqueline Mychelle. Jacquie for short. So, I'll adhere to her wishes."

"That's such a pretty name. I'm sure she's happy with it."

Just then Jacquie cooed in her sleep. She was dreaming of the beautiful woman she met with the lovely smile.

1:3:8:XI-A:B:D:E:F:G:H

Dedicated to my baby sister Jackie Michelle.

Theories of Death and the Afterlife

As a retired soldier who has witnessed the stark reality of mortality on numerous occasions, there exists a unique perspective on death that combines a stoic numbness with a profound curiosity about what lies beyond our earthly existence. Having faced the fragility of life in the midst of conflict, I have become captivated by the enigma of the afterlife. This curiosity, fueled by a desire to comprehend the deeper dimensions of existence, propelled me into an in-depth exploration of various theories surrounding what follows life's final moments.

In the realm of scientific theories, I find solace in the rational exploration of the afterlife. The concept of quantum immortality, rooted in the principles of quantum mechanics, intrigues my analytical mind. The idea that consciousness might persist in parallel realities, even after the cessation of life in one universe, offers a glimmer of hope and continuity. This scientific perspective becomes a source of intellectual engagement and provides a framework that aligns with my disciplined approach to understanding complex phenomena.

Turning to religious theories, I seek comfort in the rich tapestry of beliefs that have provided solace to countless individuals throughout history. The promise of an afterlife, whether in the form of heavenly rewards, spiritual evolution, or reunions with loved ones, becomes a beacon of hope amid the grim experiences of war. Being accustomed to the discipline of faith and the camaraderie it fosters, I find resonance in the idea that life's sacrifices may lead to a higher purpose or a divine destination. This religious perspective, while rooted in faith, offers a sense of purpose and continuity that complements mine and many other soldiers' understanding of duty and sacrifice.

Yet, it is the exploration of near-death experiences (NDEs) that strikes a chord with the me on a deeply personal level. Having faced mortality in the crucible of conflict, I identify with the narratives of those who have stood at the threshold of death and returned. The common elements of NDEs, such as the tunnel of light and encounters with deceased loved ones, resonate with my experiences of life's fragility and the emotional weight of camaraderie. I see in NDEs not just a glimpse into the afterlife but a testament to the resilience of the human spirit in the face of mortality.

Motivated by this profound connection to the subject matter, I embarked on a journey of research and contemplation. The anthology of life's final moments and the moments thereafter becomes a personal quest to reconcile the harsh realities witnessed on the battlefield, at home, and in everyday life, with the timeless questions about the nature of existence. Through the lens of scientific inquiry, religious faith, and the narratives of near-death experiences, I sought to weave a tapestry that honors the sacrifices of those who have faced the ultimate unknown. In this literary endeavor, I not only delved into the theories surrounding the afterlife but also crafted a narrative that explored the intersection of duty, mortality, and the enduring human spirit.

The theories about what happens when a person moves on can be complex and varied, reflecting the diverse beliefs and perspectives held by individuals, groups, communities, and cultures around the world. I truly hope that after reading through them all that you as the reader gain a new perspective on the afterlife and what may await you. Yes, some theories do seem ridiculous, far-fetched, and downright insane, but all of the theories provided are among the top theories worldwide. Whether there is truth to any of them is yours to decide and yours to believe, but like myself, you can respect the knowledge gained.

Religious Theories

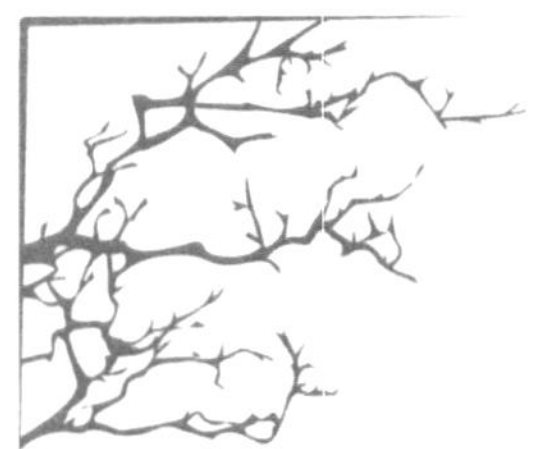

Religious theories propose the existence of an afterlife, where the soul or spirit of the deceased person goes to either heaven, hell, purgatory, or similar realms under various names, based on their actions during their lifetime. In these places they will likely be judged, tortured, face trials, or live on perpetually in bliss and happiness. The decisions determining these factors are usually from the events that the individuals did while still alive. Only certain circumstances occur on occasion in text that allow for individuals to change their outcomes. Spiritual beliefs also propose the possibility of reincarnation, where a person's soul is reborn into a new body and begins a new life, or the transfer of energy to another form, such as a plant or animal. Some cultures believe in a dream-like state after death, where people can continue to experience life but in a different form. The list below does not cover all religious theories, but it does cover many of the widest believed theories worldwide.

The concept of the afterlife is deeply embedded in the spiritual and religious narratives of diverse cultures and belief systems across the globe. Theologians, philosophers, and religious scholars have grappled with questions surrounding what happens to an individual's essence or soul after death, offering various interpretations that are often shaped by cultural contexts, sacred texts, and spiritual teachings.

Many major world religions, such as Christianity, Islam, Hinduism, Buddhism, and Judaism, incorporate the notion of an afterlife into their core doctrines. In Christianity, for instance, beliefs about heaven, hell, and resurrection are grounded in biblical teachings. The Quran, central to Islam, details the Day of Judgment and the subsequent assignment of souls to either heaven or hell based on one's deeds. Hinduism incorporates the cycle of reincarnation, where the soul undergoes a series of rebirths until reaching moksha, a state of liberation from the cycle.

Islamic traditions also describe the intricate details of the afterlife, including the crossing of the Sirat bridge and the presentation of deeds on the Day of Judgment. Meanwhile, Indigenous belief systems often incorporate ideas of ancestral spirits and a connection between the living and the deceased.

Buddhism, while not subscribing to a traditional notion of a personal soul, posits a continuation of consciousness through various forms of rebirth until attaining Nirvana. In ancient Egyptian mythology, the journey through the afterlife was intricately tied to the weighing of the heart against the feather of Ma'at, determining one's fate.

These diverse religious afterlife theories reflect humanity's profound curiosity and spiritual quest to understand the mysteries beyond the realms of our earthly existence. The following list explores twelve distinct theories from various perspectives, offering a glimpse into the richness and complexity of beliefs surrounding what occurs after the cessation of biological life.

1. **Afterlife in Heaven, Hell, or Purgatory**: Many religions posit an afterlife where the soul faces judgment and is sent to either a place of eternal bliss (heaven), punishment (hell), or undergoes purification or waiting on judgment (purgatory).
2. **Reincarnation**: This belief suggests that after death, the soul is reborn into a new body, continuing its journey through different lifetimes.
3. **Resurrection**: Some religious traditions teach that after death, a person's body will be restored to life, either in its original form or a new one.
4. **Afterlife Dimensions**: Certain spiritual beliefs propose that after death, a person's consciousness may traverse other dimensions or planes of existence.
5. **Spiritual Evolution**: Some religious and philosophical traditions suggest that after death, a person's soul or consciousness may continue to evolve or learn.
6. **Karma and Spiritual Evolution**: Some belief systems tie the afterlife to the concept of karma, where a person's deeds in life influence their spiritual evolution or the circumstances of their next existence.
7. **Ancestor Worship**: Certain cultural and religious practices involve

honoring and communicating with the spirits of deceased ancestors, suggesting a continued presence or influence.

8. **Judgment and Reckoning**: In addition to afterlife destinations, some religions emphasize a judgment or reckoning, where individuals account for their actions before moving on to the next phase.

9. **Mystical Union with the Divine**: Mystical traditions posits that after death, the soul may achieve a union with the divine or a cosmic consciousness.

10. **Messianic or Apocalyptic Beliefs**: Some religions hold that after death, individuals may play a role in future messianic or apocalyptic events, influencing the ultimate fate of the world.

11. **Astral Projection Theory**: According to this theory, the soul separates from the body at death and enters a new realm of existence, where it can interact with other souls.

12. **Spiritual Evolution Theory/The Levels Theory**: Some religious and philosophical traditions teach that after death, a person's soul or consciousness may continue to evolve or learn in some way.

Scientific Theories

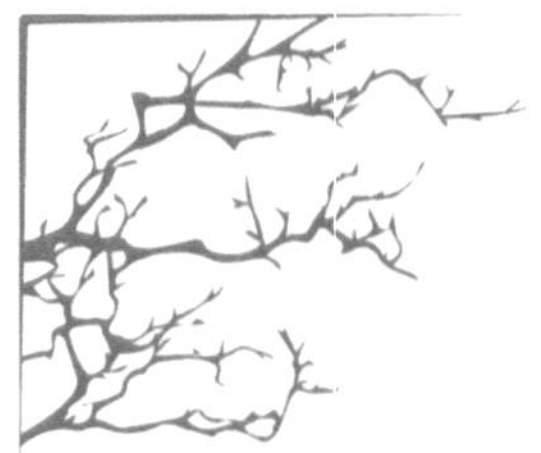

Scientifically, death is seen as the cessation of all bodily functions, including brain activity, which means that consciousness and awareness are no longer possible. Philosophically, some people believe in the idea of nothingness, where after death, we simply cease to exist and there is no afterlife or continuation of consciousness. The cosmic recycling theory proposes that when a person dies, their body returns to the earth, where it becomes part of the ecosystem and is recycled into other life forms. Finally, some people believe in the simulation theory, which suggests that our reality is a simulation, and when a person dies, they simply exit the simulation and return to the "real" world.

Scientific exploration of the afterlife delves into realms of consciousness, quantum mechanics, and the fundamental nature of reality. Rooted in disciplines like neuroscience, physics, and philosophy, these theories emerge from attempts to understand existence beyond the confines of biological life.

Neuroscience grapples with the intricate relationship between the brain and consciousness. Some propose that consciousness is an emergent property of the brain, suggesting that when the brain ceases to function, consciousness dissolves into nothingness. Exploring this avenue, David Eagleman's work in "Incognito: The Secret Lives of the Brain" delves into the complexities of the brain and its implications for consciousness.

Quantum mechanics introduces intriguing ideas about the persistence of consciousness. The concept of quantum immortality, explored by Max Tegmark in "Our Mathematical Universe," speculates that in a multiverse, one's consciousness may continue to exist in parallel realities, contributing to the notion of quantum immortality.

Information theory, as applied to consciousness, forms another scientific perspective. Giulio Tononi's "Phi: A Voyage from the Brain to the Soul" delves into the Integrated Information Theory, proposing that consciousness arises from the integrated complexity of information processing within the brain. When the brain dies, this information may disperse, influencing the broader informational landscape.

The multiverse hypothesis, discussed by Brian Greene in "The Hidden Reality," opens avenues for speculating about the continuity of consciousness. In a multiverse, alternate realities might provide frameworks for the persistence of individual consciousness or its echoes.

These scientific theories navigate the boundaries of our understanding, blending the empirical and the speculative. As we explore the mysteries of consciousness and existence, these theories contribute to a broader scientific conversation, challenging traditional paradigms and encouraging us to rethink the nature of life, death, and what may lie beyond. The ensuing list delves into thirteen specific theories within this scientific framework, offering a glimpse into the diverse ways in which science seeks to unravel the enigma of the afterlife.

I. **Nothingness**: Philosophical perspectives propose that death results in the absolute end of a person's existence, with no afterlife or continuation of consciousness.

II. **Energy Transfer/The Tree Theory**: Certain scientific theories propose that the energy animating a person's body is released and dispersed back into the environment after death.

III. **Emergent Property**: Some scientists suggest that consciousness may be an emergent property of the brain, ceasing to exist when the brain dies.

IV. **Quantum Physics**: There is speculation in scientific circles that consciousness may be a fundamental aspect of the universe, raising the possibility of its continuation after the body's death.

V. **Biological Decomposition**: Beyond the cessation of bodily functions, scientific theories highlight the natural process of biological decomposition as the body returns to the elemental components, leading to the end of consciousness and awareness.

VI. **Quantum Immortality**: A speculative concept in quantum physics suggests that an individual's consciousness might continue to exist in some parallel universes, creating a form of "quantum immortality."

VII. **Information Theory of Consciousness**: Some theories propose that consciousness is a form of information processing, and after death, this information disperses into the environment.

VIII. **Multiverse Hypothesis**: Drawing from speculative physics, some propose that consciousness might persist in alternate universes within a multiverse after the death of the physical body.

IX. **Neurological Echo**: Some theories speculate that echoes of a person's consciousness may persist in the collective memory of society or through recorded information, influencing future generations.

X. **The Dream Theory**: Some cultures believe that our existence is that of a great dreamer, upon death we can continue to experience life, albeit in a different form. However, upon the awakening of the dreamer our reality simply no longer exists.

XI. **The Ghost Theory/The Paranormal Theory**: Some people believe that after death, a person's spirit/energy can remain on Earth and haunt their loved ones or the places they used to frequent. Evidence suggests such spirits/energies are either trapped between worlds, living a certain event on repeat, or remain due to unfinished business.

XII. **The Simulation Theory**: This theory suggests that our reality is a simulation, and when a person dies, they simply exit the simulation and return to the "real" world.

XIII. **The Never-Ending Life Theory**: The never-ending life theory is one of the most unique on the list. This claims that when you die you are immediately reborn into your life again without any memory of the life you had just led before.

Near Death Experiences

Personally experienced accounts have brought on additional insight into what potentially occurs at death. Many accounts of seeing a white light, long halls, and hearing voices and music have been recorded over many years from people that have been saved from near death experiences. Additionally, others have recounted floating above their bodies, or being somewhere else entirely and seeing something happening at the same time, or even having a glimpse of the future. Near death experiences may not have prompted the interest into the paranormal, but it is likely these experiences initially lead people to start believing in a realm that overlapped our own where the ghosts of our loved ones or other spirits of the deceased can remain on Earth and haunt their tormentors or the places they used to frequent.

Near-death experiences (NDEs) offer a fascinating and often profound window into the mysteries surrounding consciousness, life, and the potential realms beyond our immediate sensory perception. These experiences, reported by individuals who have come close to death, share common elements such as a bright light, feelings of peace, and a sense of detachment from the physical body. The scientific and philosophical exploration of NDEs delves into understanding the nature of consciousness, the brain's role in these experiences, and their implications for our understanding of existence.

At the heart of near-death experience theories lies the question of what happens to consciousness when the body is on the brink of death. Psychologist and philosopher Raymond A. Moody, Jr., in his groundbreaking work "Life After Life," was among the pioneers to systematically document and analyze the common features of NDEs. These include the sensation of leaving the body, moving through a tunnel toward a light, and encountering deceased loved ones.

The medical and scientific community has also engaged in the study of NDEs, with cardiologist Pim van Lommel contributing significantly to the discourse. In "Consciousness Beyond Life," van Lommel explores cases of cardiac arrest patients who reported NDEs, providing a medical perspective on these seemingly otherworldly experiences. The book delves into the potential implications of NDEs for our understanding of consciousness and the mind-brain relationship.

Beyond the scientific perspective, individuals who have undergone near-death experiences often share their personal narratives, providing insights into the emotional, psychological, and spiritual transformations that can result from these encounters. Anita Moorjani's "Dying to Be Me" is a poignant autobiographical account where she recounts her near-death experience and the subsequent healing and profound shifts in her perspective on life.

These theories and narratives collectively contribute to a multifaceted exploration of near-death experiences, challenging us to consider the nature of consciousness, the limits of our understanding, and the potential existence of realms beyond the confines of our physical existence. The subsequent list outlines eleven distinct near-death experience theories, offering a glimpse into the richness and diversity of perspectives surrounding this intriguing phenomenon.

A. **Tunnel of Light**: Many people report moving through a dark tunnel toward a bright light, often described as a warm and inviting presence.

B. **Out-of-Body Experience (OBE)**: Some individuals claim to have observed their own bodies from a vantage point outside themselves during a medical emergency.

C. **Life Review**: People often describe a rapid and vivid review of significant life events, accompanied by a sense of judgment or understanding of the consequences of their actions.

D. **Encounters with Deceased Loved Ones**: Some report meeting deceased friends or family members who offer comfort, guidance, or encouragement.

E. **Feelings of Peace and Love**: A common element involves experiencing overwhelming feelings of peace, love, and acceptance beyond what can be expressed in earthly terms.

F. **Meeting Spiritual Beings**: Individuals may encounter angelic or spiritual beings, entities that emanate wisdom and convey a sense of cosmic understanding.

G. **Entering Another Realm**: Some near-death experiences describe entering a different realm or dimension, often characterized by vibrant colors, indescribable landscapes, or a heightened sense of reality.

H. **Communication with a Divine Presence**: A significant number of people report encountering a divine or supreme being, which may be perceived as God, a higher power, or a universal consciousness.

I. **Life-Altering Insights**: Near-death experiences can bring profound insights, a heightened awareness of interconnectedness, and a renewed sense of purpose or mission in life.

J. **Reluctance to Return**: Many individuals express reluctance or disappointment when they are brought back to life, having felt the allure of the afterlife or a different dimension.

K. **Afterlife Dimensions Theory**: Some spiritual beliefs propose that after death, a person's consciousness may travel to other dimensions or planes of existence.

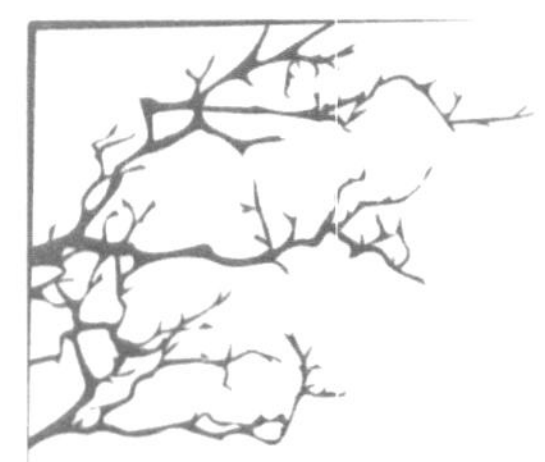

References

Abdul Husayn Dastaghaib Shirazi, Sayyid. "Barzakh (Purgatory) - the Stage between This World and the Hereafter ..." *Barzakh (Purgatory) - The Stage Between This World and the Hereafter*, Al-Islam.org, www.al-islam.org/hereafter-maad-sayyid-abdul-husayn-dastghaib-shirazi/barzakh-purgatory-stage-between-world-and

Kiprop, Joseph. "What Are Wiccan Beliefs?" *WorldAtlas*, WorldAtlas, 4 Oct. 2017, https://www.worldatlas.com/articles/what-are-wiccan-beliefs.html

Order of Bards, Ovates & Druids. "Druid: The Teachings, Beliefs & History of Druidism: Obod." *Order of Bards, Ovates & Druids*, Order of Bards, Ovates & Druids, 11 Jan. 2022, https://druidry.org/

Panda, Conscious. "What Happens When We Die? Theories of the Afterlife." *Conscious Panda*, 8 Jan. 2021, https://consciouspanda.com/what-happens-when-we-die-theories-of-the-afterlife/

Pickover, Clifford A. *Death and the Afterlife: A Chronological Journey from Cremation to Quantum Resurrection*. Sterling New York, an Imprint of Sterling Publishing, 2015.

About the Publisher

Echoes of Service is more than just a publishing company; it's a platform dedicated to amplifying the voices of veterans, first responders, and their families through storytelling. Founded by a former Special Forces veteran with a passion for writing and a mission to empower others, Echoes of Service provides a unique opportunity for individuals to share their stories and experiences with the world.

At Echoes of Service, we believe that every voice deserves to be heard, and every story has the power to inspire, educate, and connect. From riveting memoirs to captivating fiction, our diverse catalog of books celebrates the richness of human experience and offers readers a glimpse into the lives of those who have served and sacrificed for others.

Driven by a commitment to authenticity and excellence, we strive to uphold the highest standards of publishing while honoring the integrity of each author's voice. Through collaboration, creativity, and community, we aim to create meaningful connections and foster understanding among readers from all walks of life.

Join us on this journey as we explore the echoes of service and celebrate the indomitable spirit of those who have dedicated their lives to serving others.

For more information about Echoes of Service, our publications, and to join our community visit https://echoesofservice.substack.com/